BABYMOUSE
BURNS RUBBER

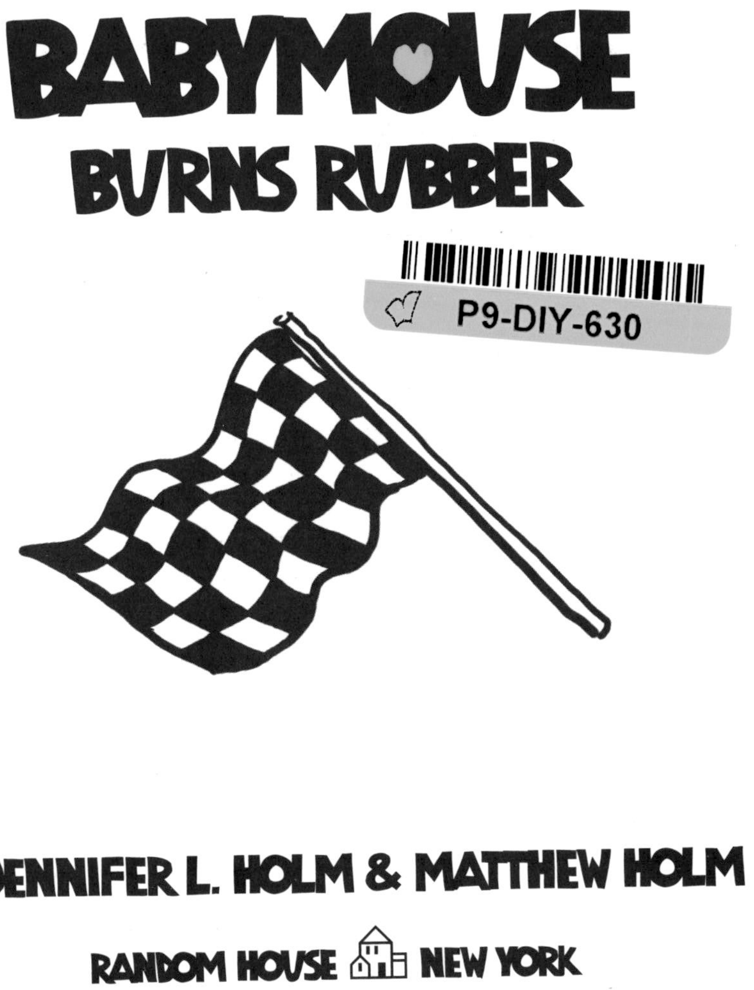

BY JENNIFER L. HOLM & MATTHEW HOLM

RANDOM HOUSE NEW YORK

I'M MAKING A PIT STOP.

Copyright © 2010 by Jennifer Holm and Matthew Holm

All rights reserved.
Published in the United States by Random House Children's Books,
a division of Random House, Inc., New York.

Random House and the colophon are registered trademarks of Random House, Inc.

Visit us on the Web! www.randomhouse.com/kids
www.babymouse.com

Educators and librarians, for a variety of teaching tools,
visit us at www.randomhouse.com/teachers

Library of Congress Cataloging-in-Publication Data
Holm, Jennifer L.
Babymouse : burns rubber / by Jennifer and Matthew Holm. — 1st ed.
    p. cm.
Summary: Babymouse's dreams of being a race car driver come true when she and
her best friend Wilson enter a soap box derby.
ISBN 978-0-375-85713-3 (trade pbk.) — ISBN 978-0-375-95713-0 (lib. bdg.)
1. Graphic novels. [1. Graphic novels. 2. Imagination—Fiction. 3. Soap box derbies—Fiction.
4. Mice—Fiction. 5. Animals—Fiction. 6. Humorous stories.]
I. Holm, Matthew. II. Title. III. Title: Burns rubber.
PZ7.7.H65Bad 2010 741.5'973—dc22 2009018819

MANUFACTURED IN MALAYSIA   10 9 8 7 6 5 4   First Edition

MORE PRAISE F

"Sassy, smart . . .
Babymouse is here
to stay."
—The Horn Book Magazine

"Young readers
will happily
fall in line."
—Kirkus Reviews

"The brother-sister creative team hits the mark
with humor, sweetness, and characters so genuine
they can pass for real kids." **—Booklist**

"Babymouse is spunky, ambitious,
and, at times, a total dweeb."
—School Library Journal

Be sure to read **all** the **BABYMOUSE** books:

#1 BABYMOUSE: Queen of the World!
#2 BABYMOUSE: Our Hero
#3 BABYMOUSE: Beach Babe
#4 BABYMOUSE: Rock Star
#5 BABYMOUSE: Heartbreaker
#6 CAMP BABYMOUSE
#7 BABYMOUSE: Skater Girl
#8 BABYMOUSE: Puppy Love
#9 BABYMOUSE: Monster Mash
#10 BABYMOUSE: The Musical
#11 BABYMOUSE: Dragonslayer
#12 BABYMOUSE: Burns Rubber

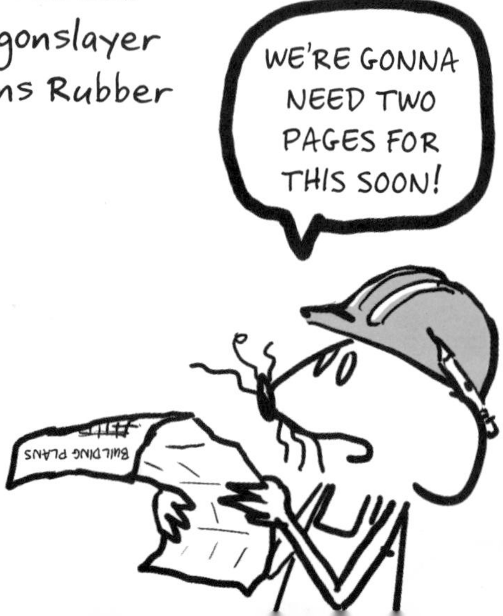
WE'RE GONNA NEED TWO PAGES FOR THIS SOON!
BUILDING PLANS

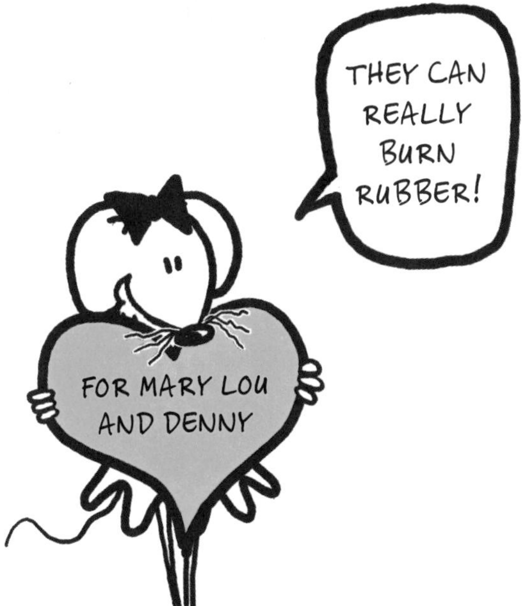
THEY CAN REALLY BURN RUBBER!
FOR MARY LOU AND DENNY

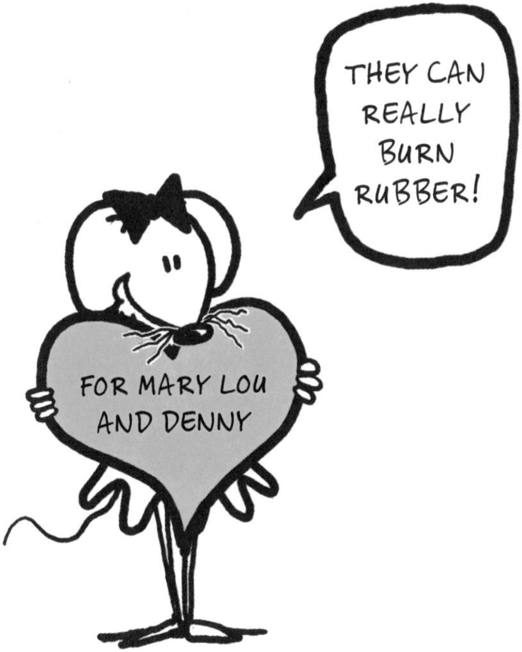
FOR MARY LOU AND DENNY
THEY CAN REALLY BURN RUBBER!

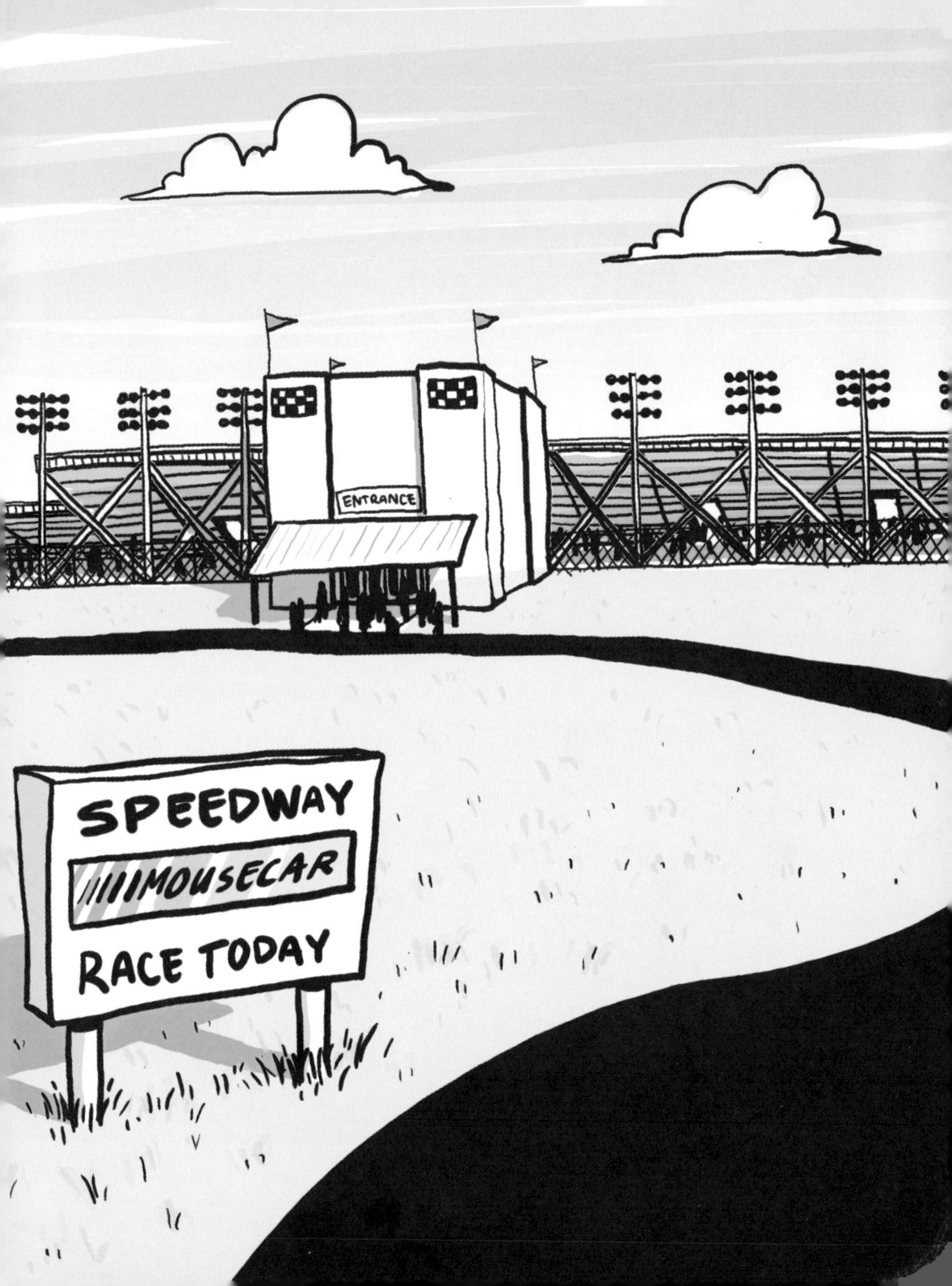
ENTRANCE
SPEEDWAY
MOUSECAR
RACE TODAY

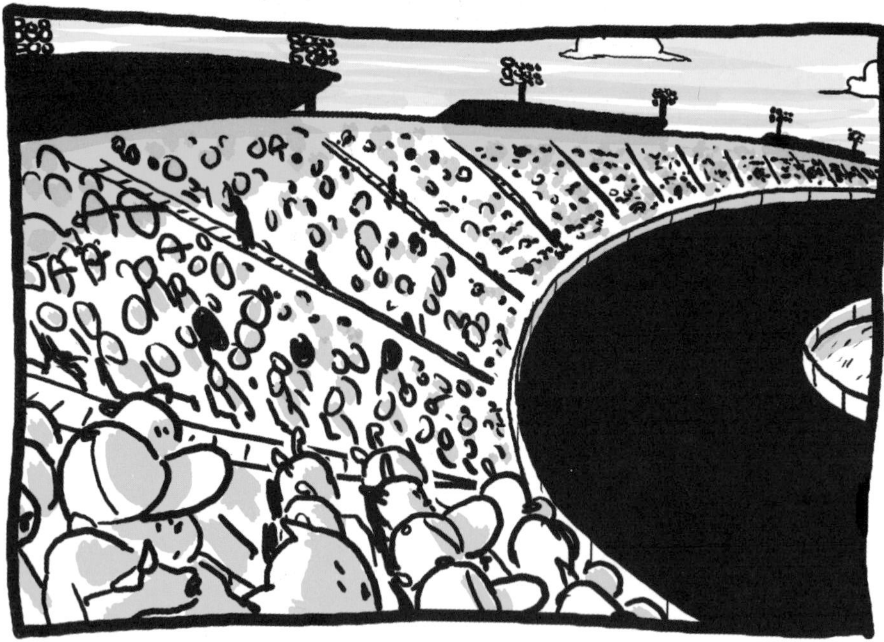

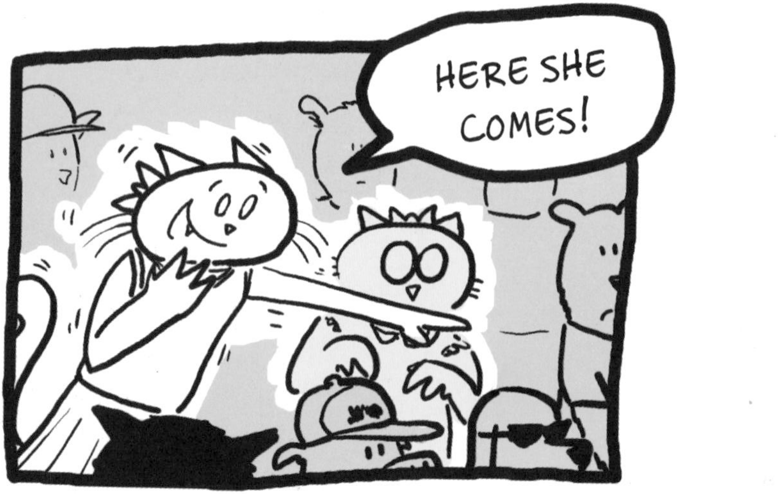
HERE SHE COMES!

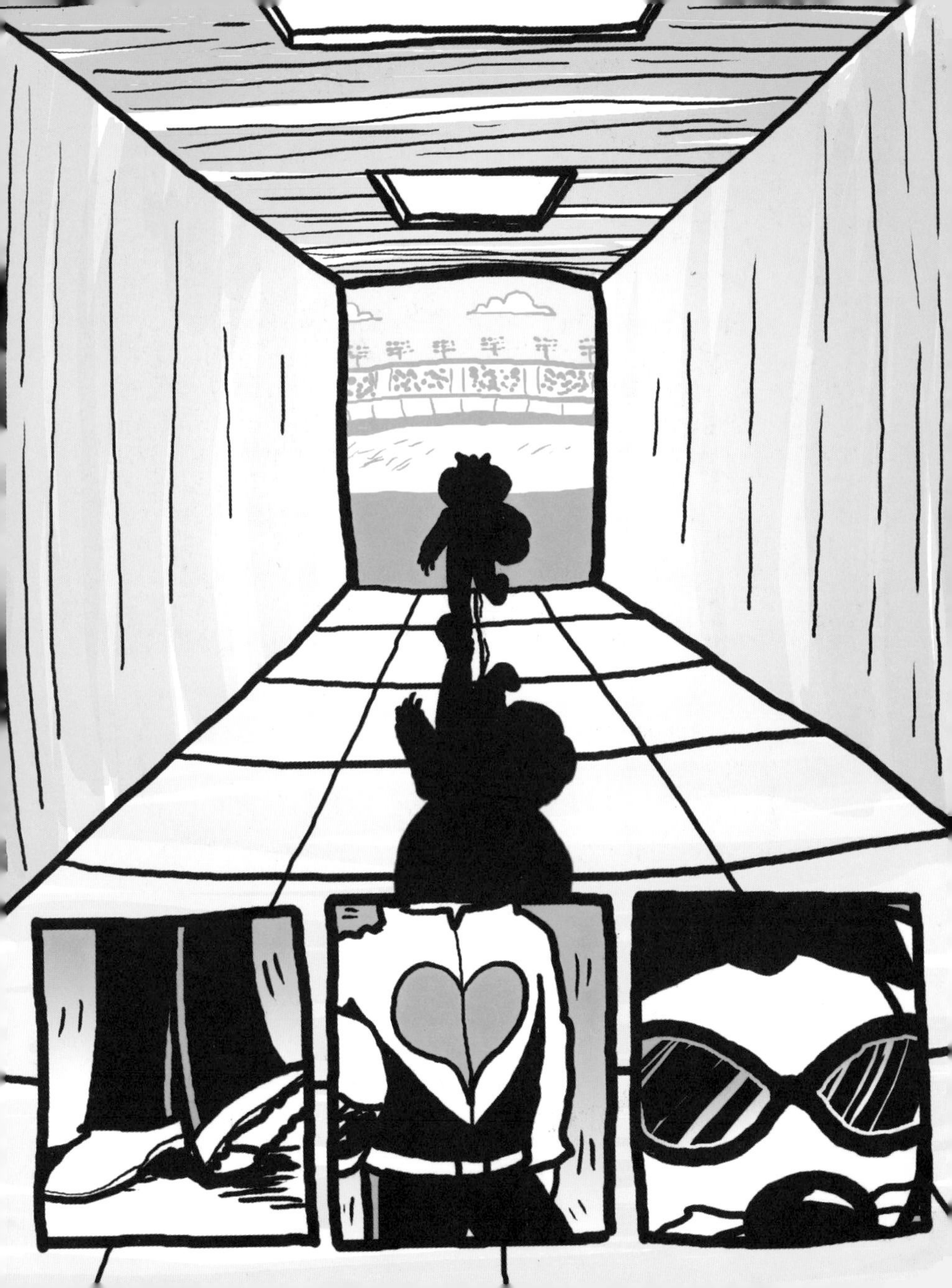

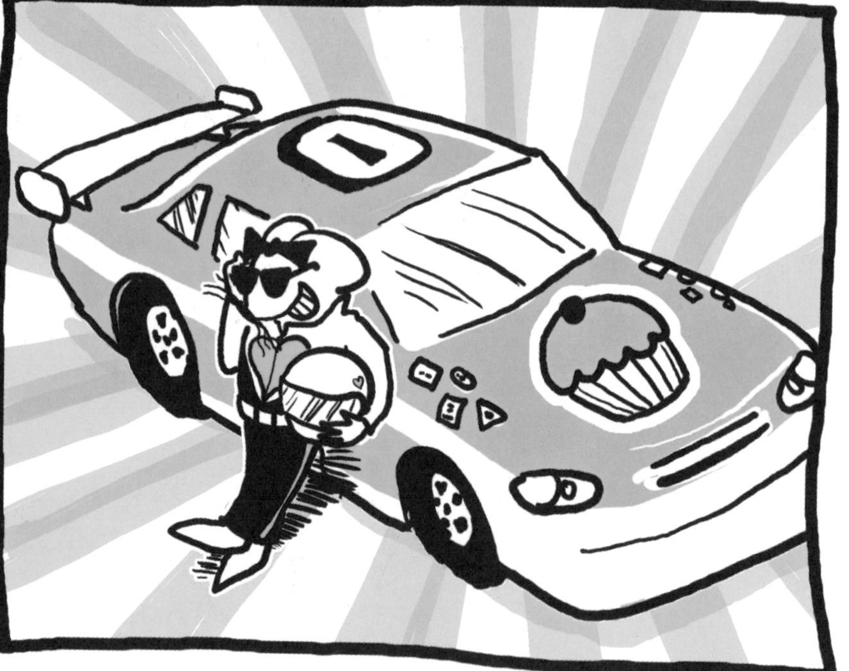

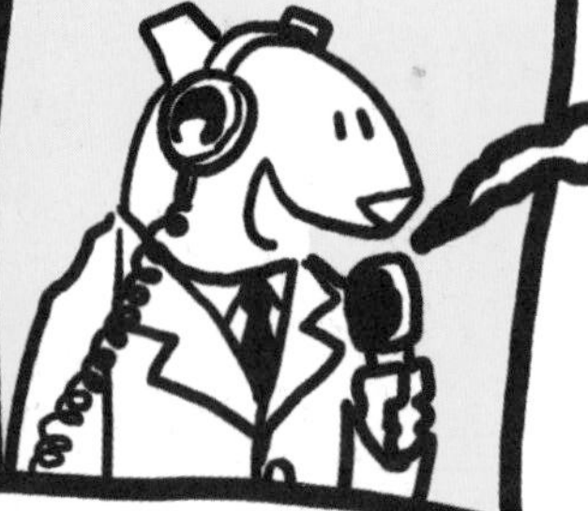

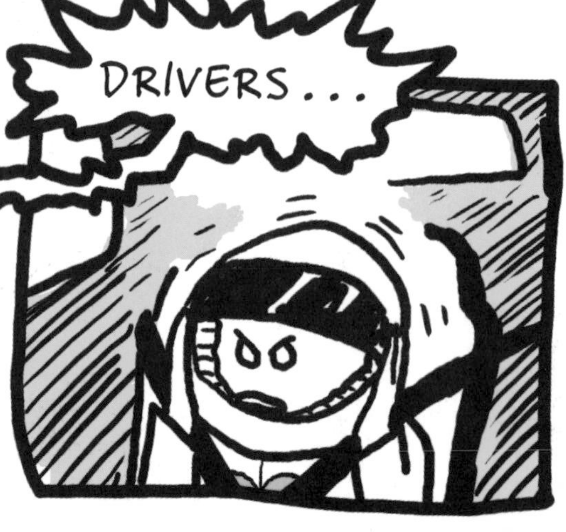
DRIVERS . . .

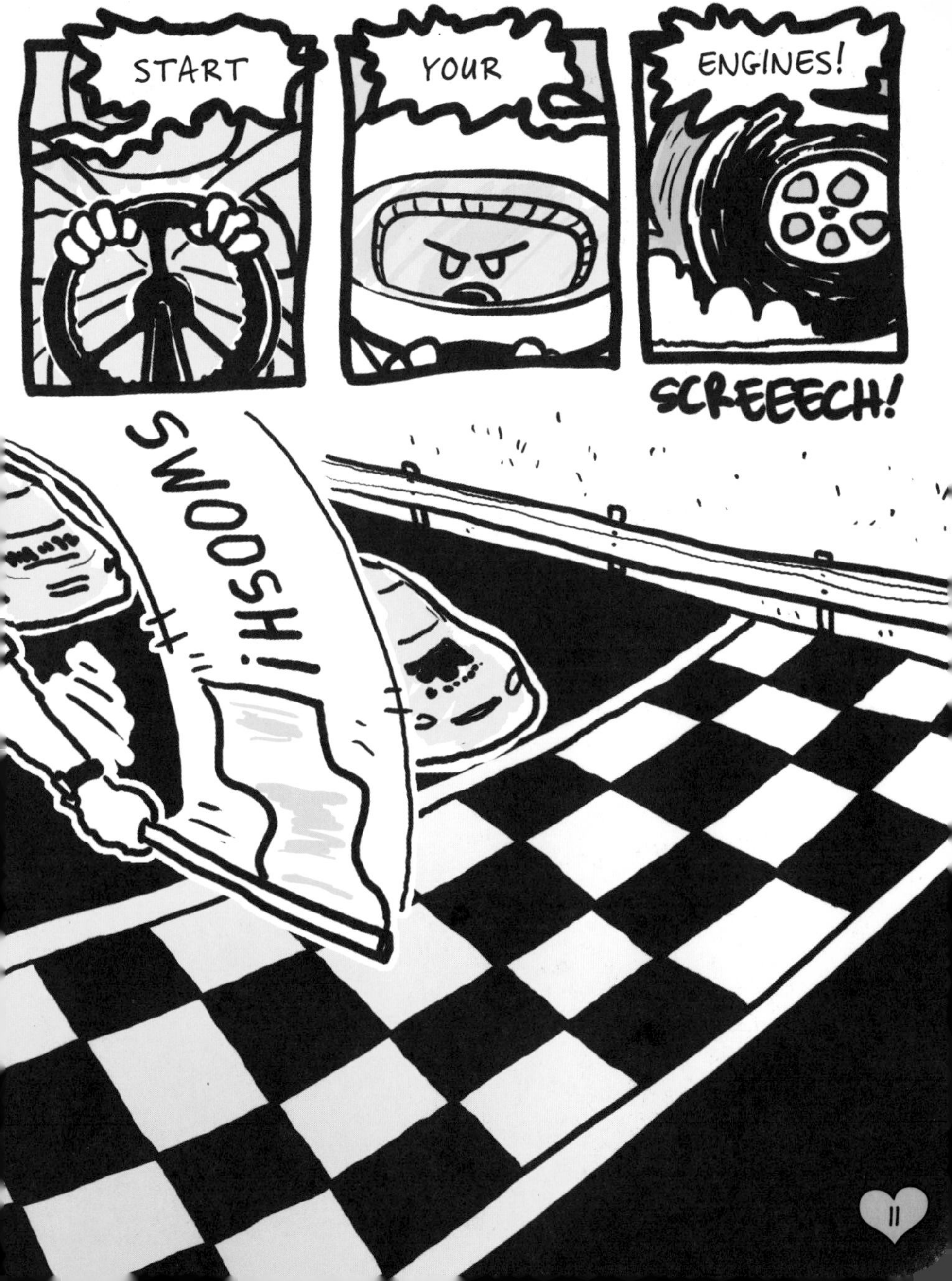
START
YOUR
ENGINES!
SCREEECH!
SWOOSH!

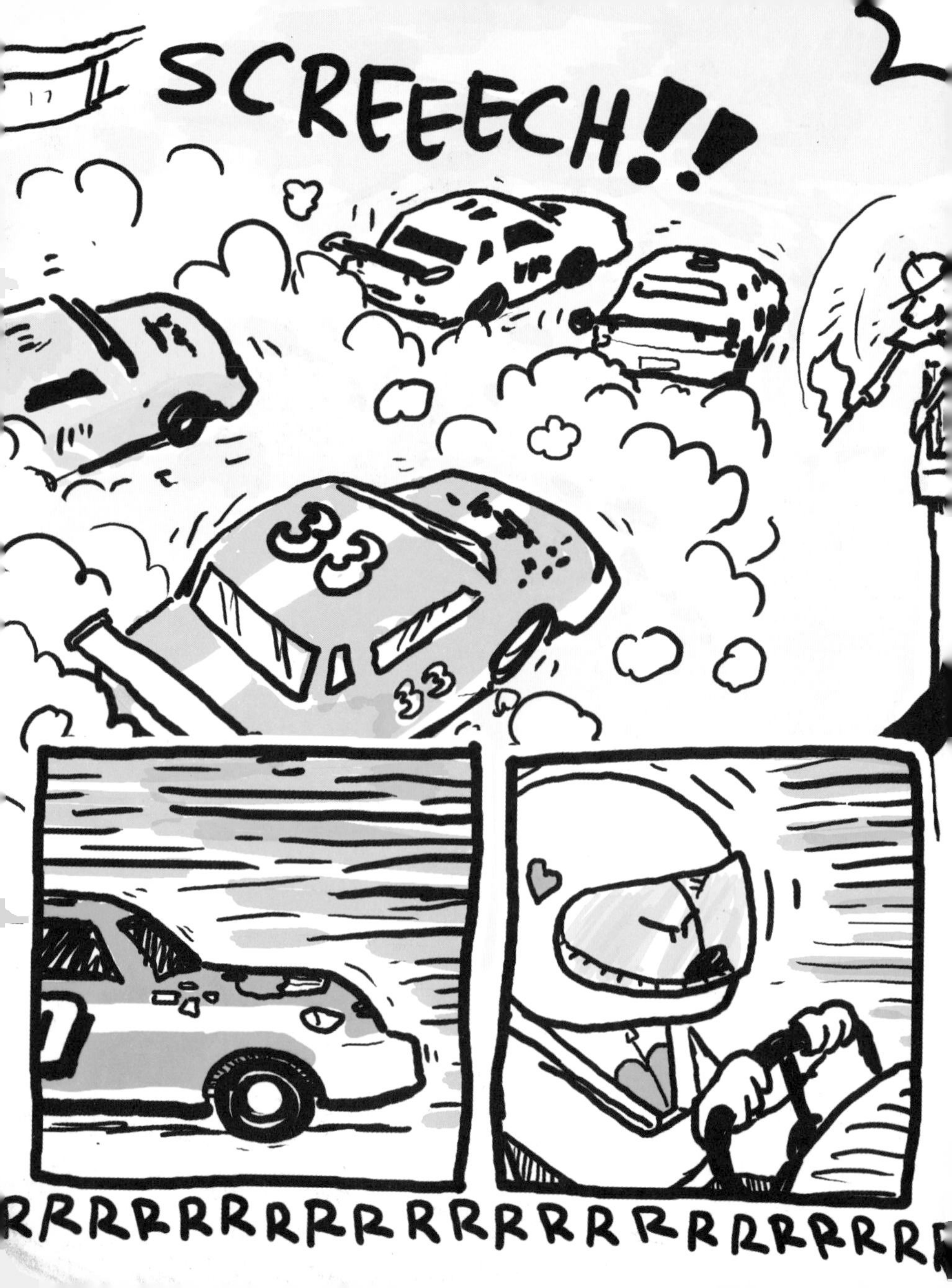
SCREEECH!!
33
33
RRRRRRRRRRRRRRRRRRRRR

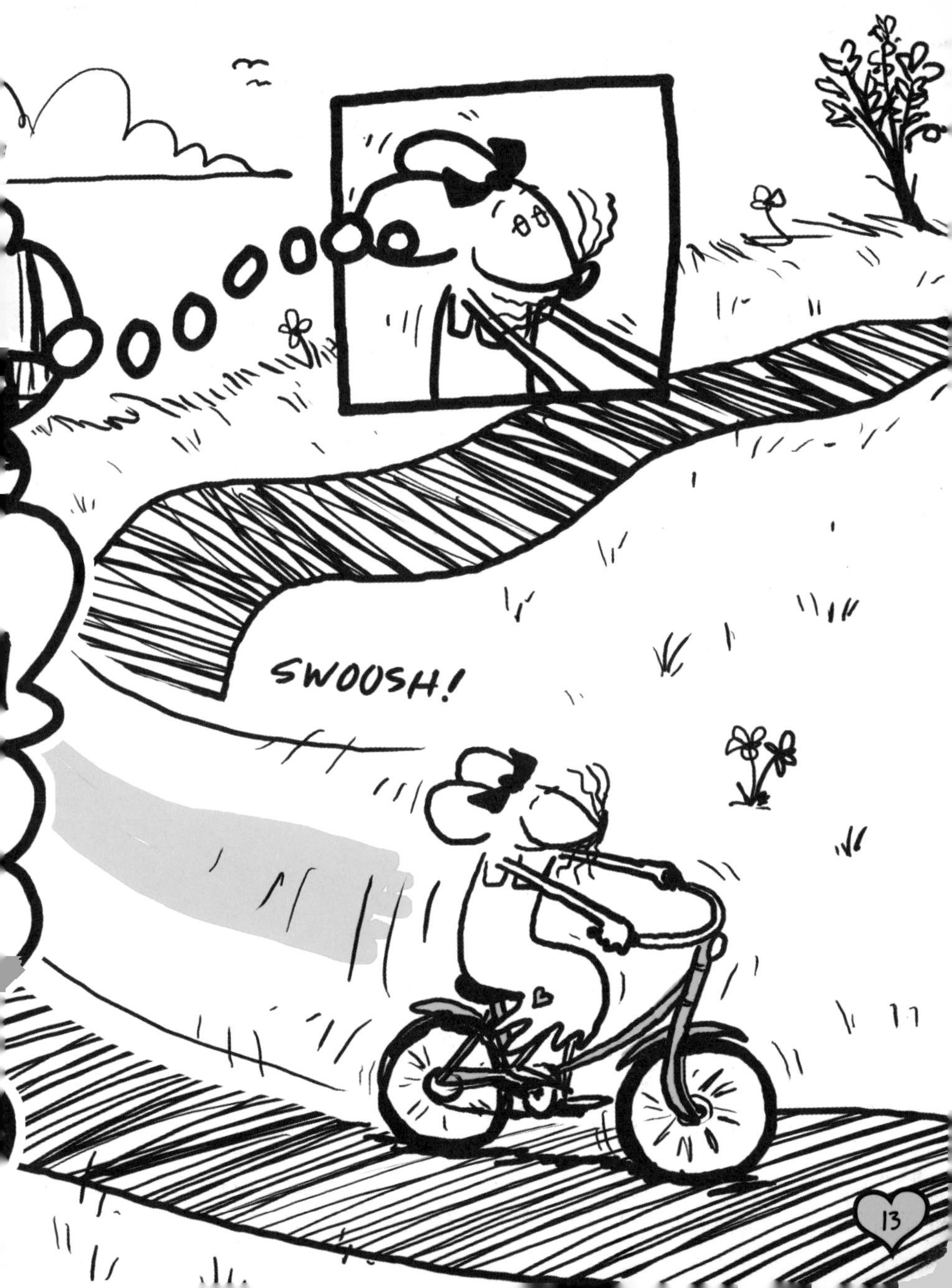
SWOOSH!

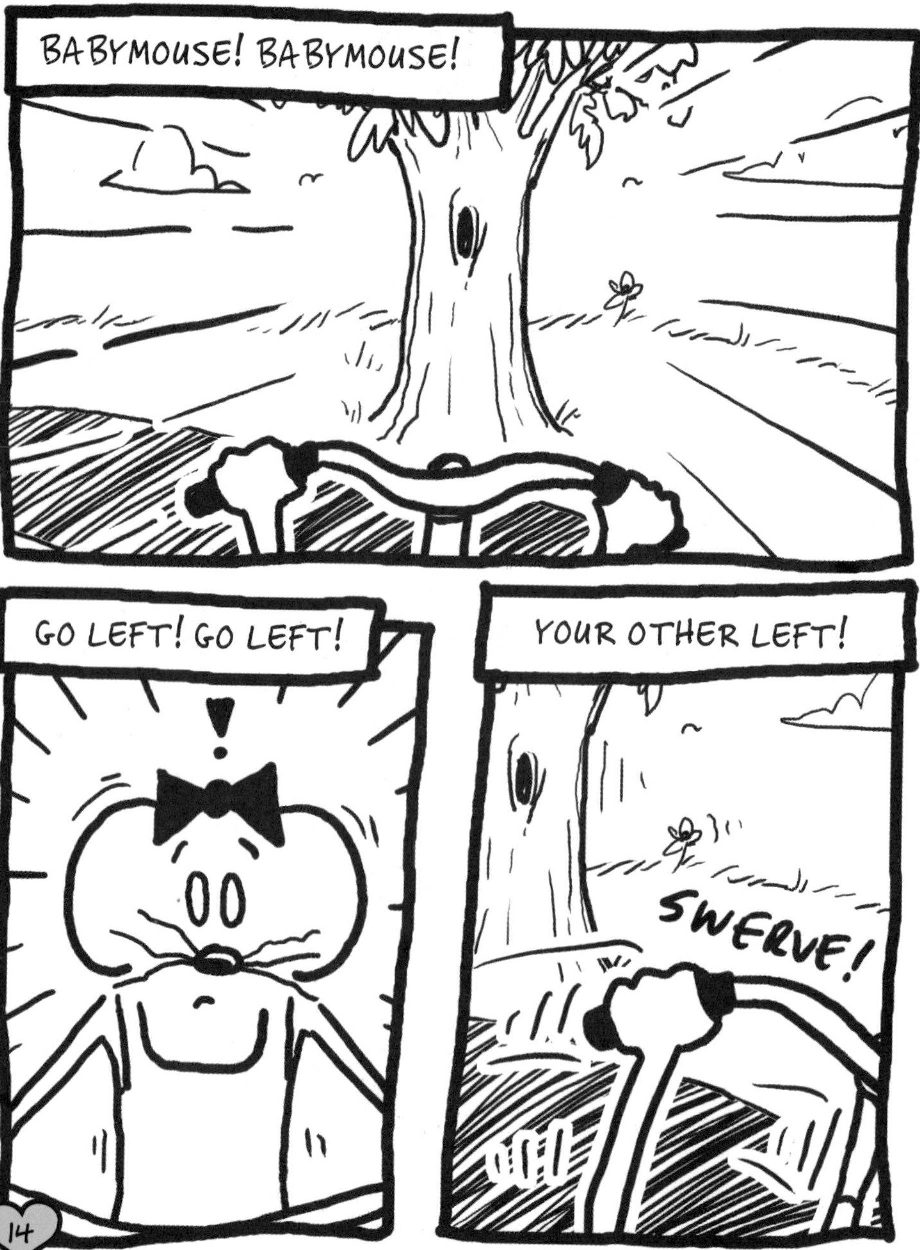
BABYMOUSE! BABYMOUSE!
GO LEFT! GO LEFT!
!
YOUR OTHER LEFT!
SWERVE!

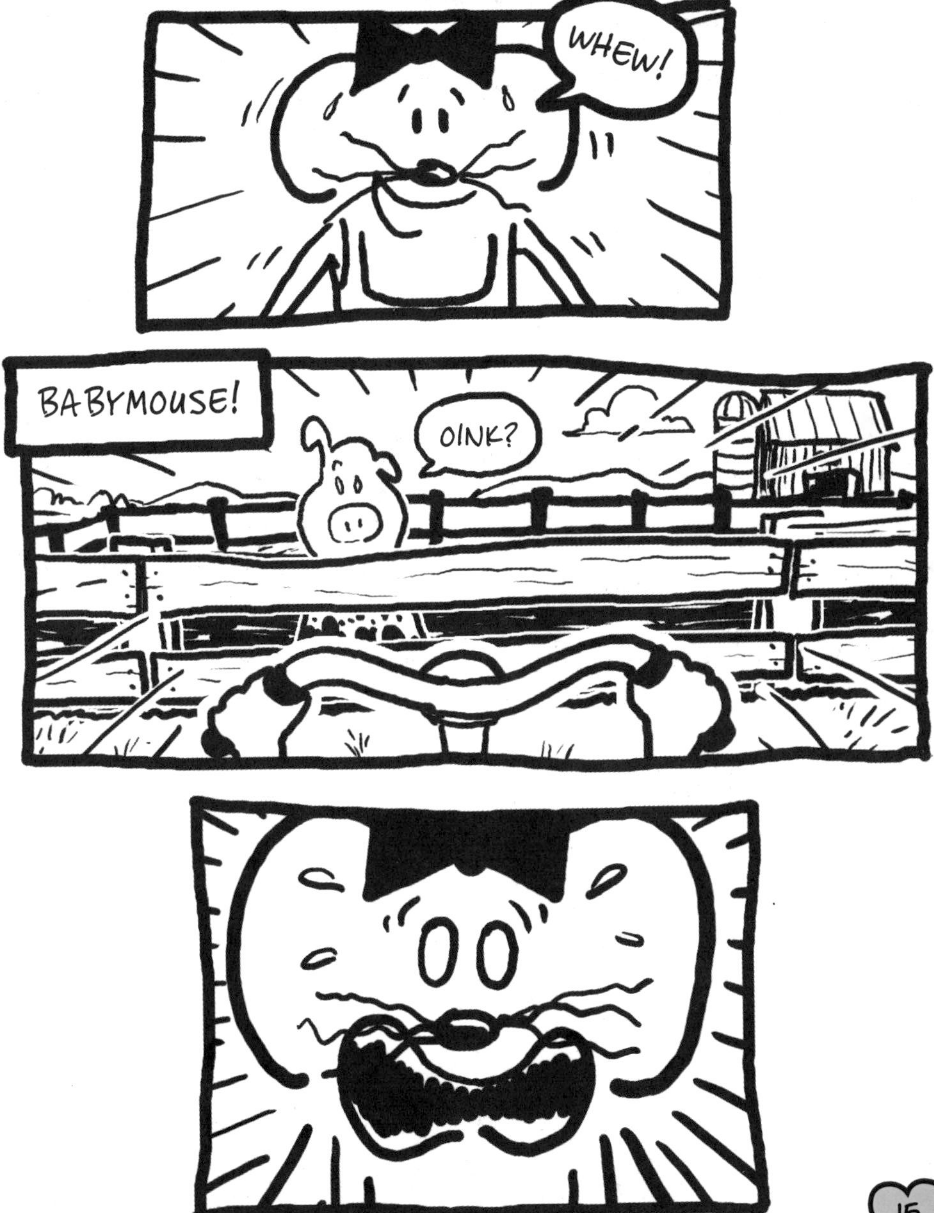
WHEW!
BABYMOUSE!
OINK?

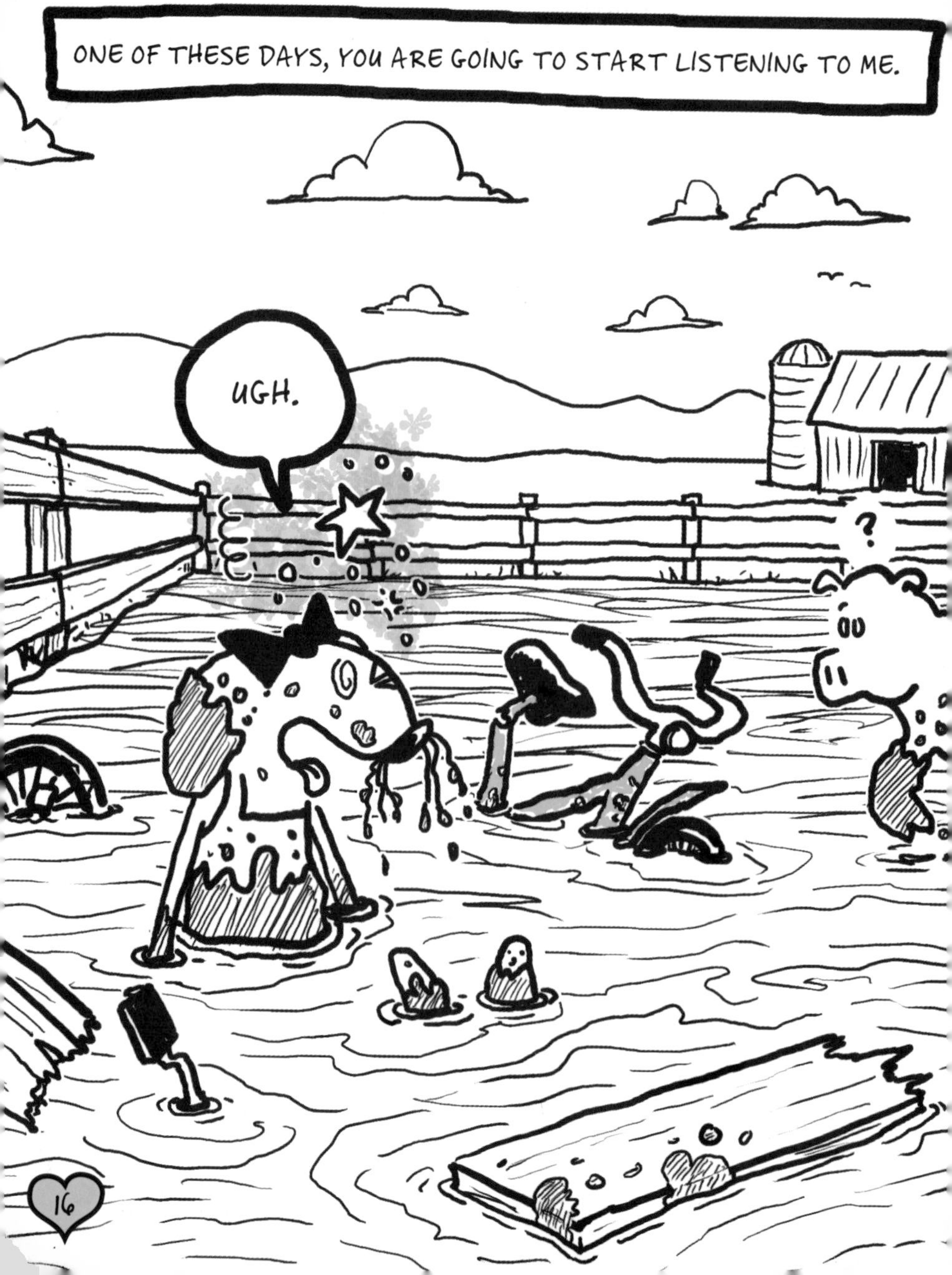
ONE OF THESE DAYS, YOU ARE GOING TO START LISTENING TO ME.
UGH.
?

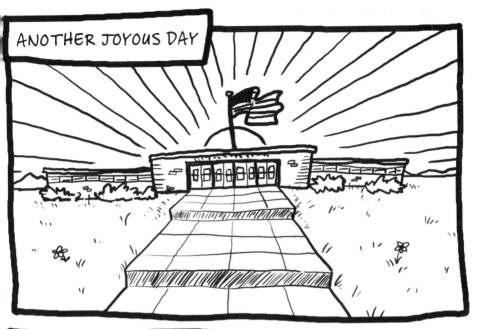

ANOTHER JOYOUS DAY

IN THE HALLOWED HALLS

LEMENTARY SCHOO

OF LEARNING.

17

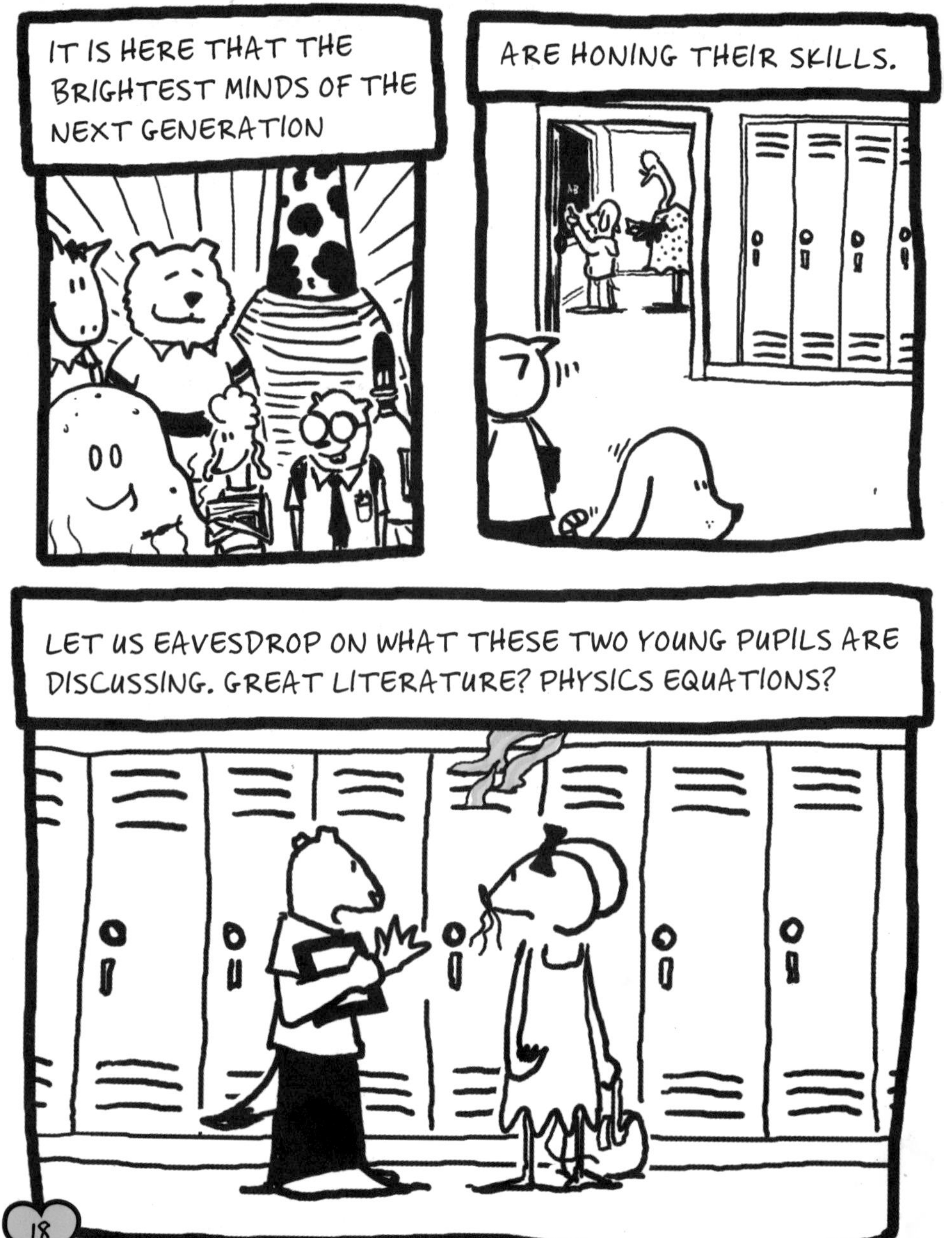
IT IS HERE THAT THE BRIGHTEST MINDS OF THE NEXT GENERATION
ARE HONING THEIR SKILLS.
LET US EAVESDROP ON WHAT THESE TWO YOUNG PUPILS ARE DISCUSSING. GREAT LITERATURE? PHYSICS EQUATIONS?

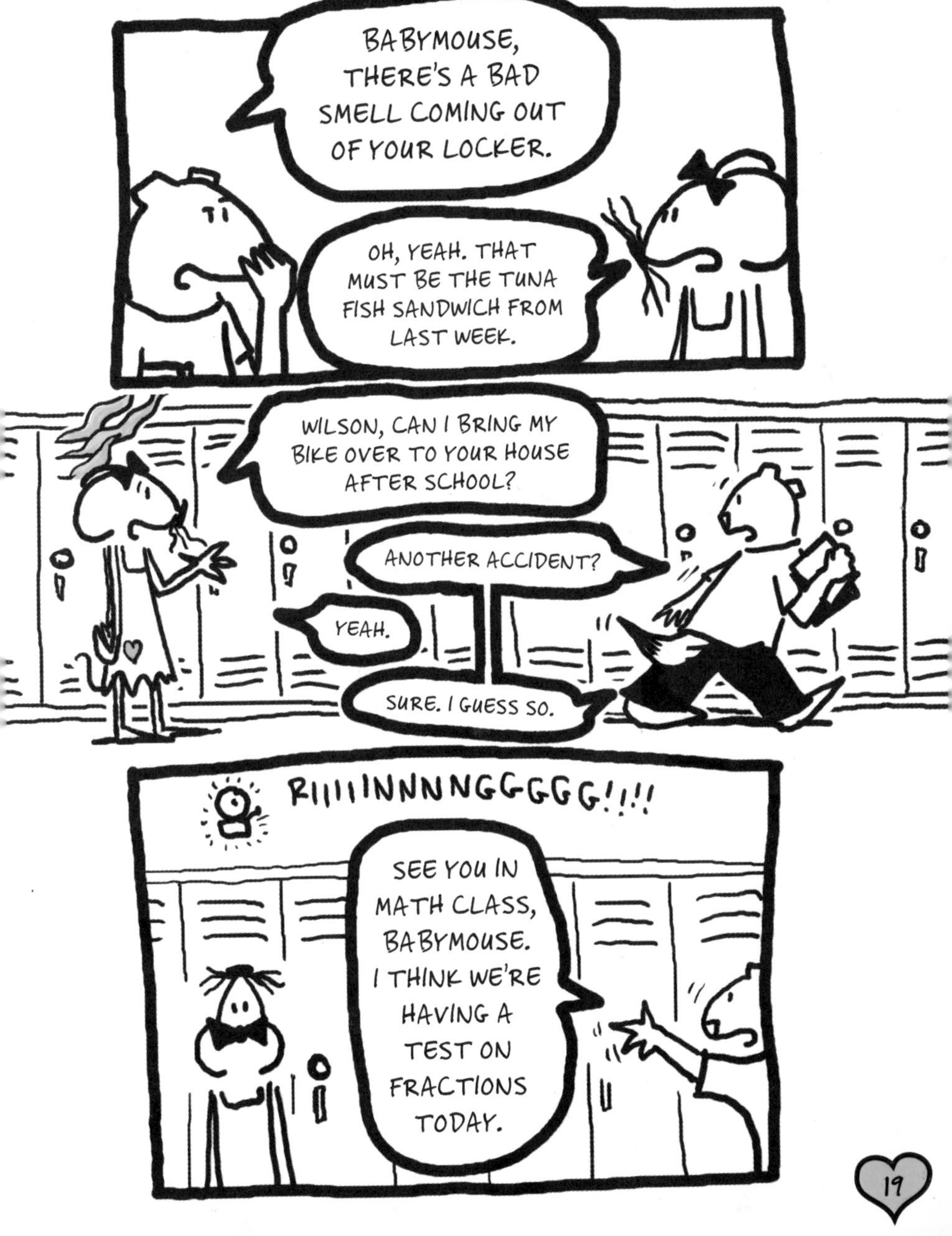
BABYMOUSE, THERE'S A BAD SMELL COMING OUT OF YOUR LOCKER.
OH, YEAH. THAT MUST BE THE TUNA FISH SANDWICH FROM LAST WEEK.
WILSON, CAN I BRING MY BIKE OVER TO YOUR HOUSE AFTER SCHOOL?
ANOTHER ACCIDENT?
YEAH.
SURE. I GUESS SO.
RIIIIINNNNGGGGG!!!!
SEE YOU IN MATH CLASS, BABYMOUSE. I THINK WE'RE HAVING A TEST ON FRACTIONS TODAY.

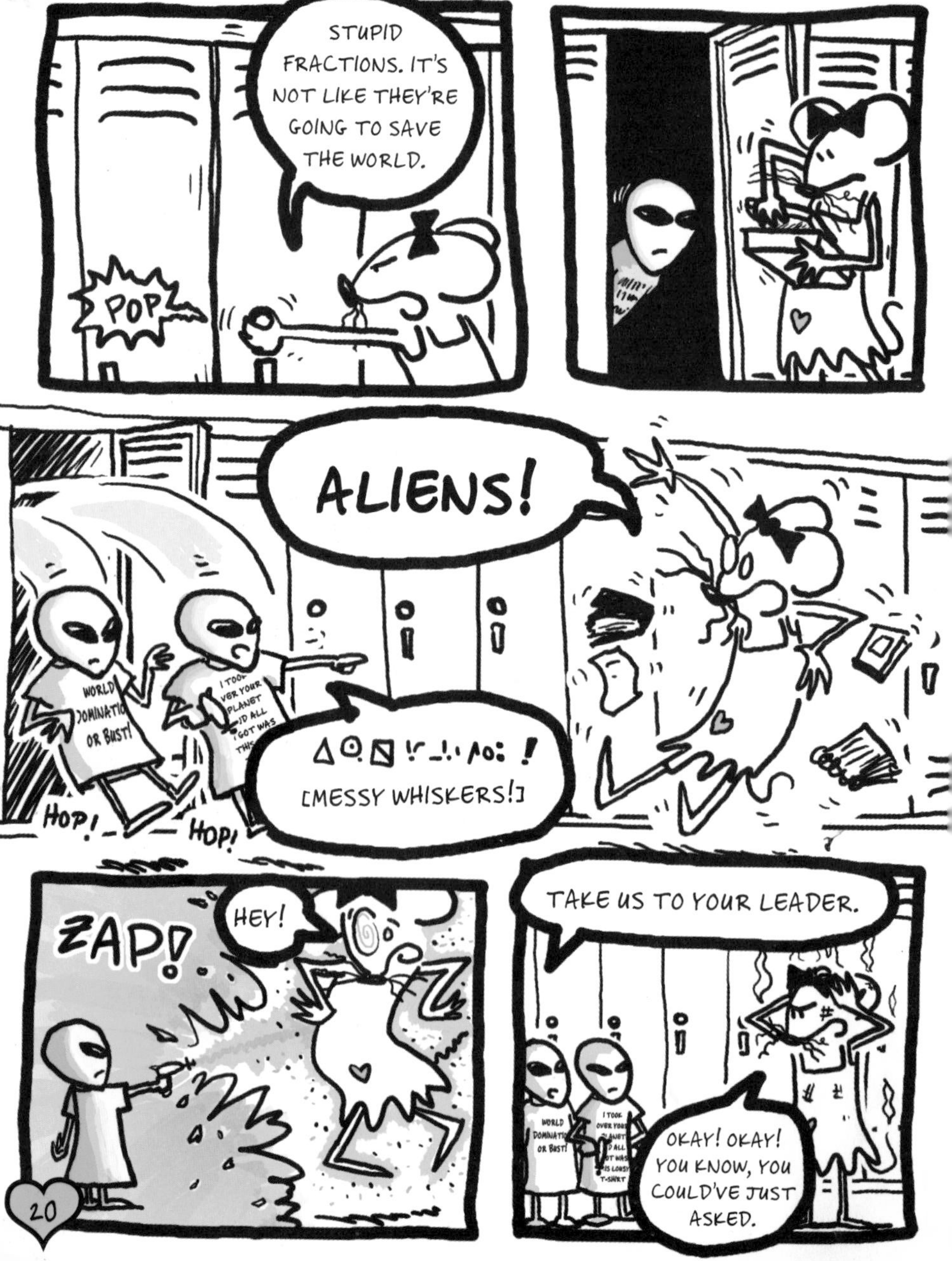
STUPID FRACTIONS. IT'S NOT LIKE THEY'RE GOING TO SAVE THE WORLD.
POP
ALIENS!
[MESSY WHISKERS!]
HOP!
HOP!
ZAP!
HEY!
TAKE US TO YOUR LEADER.
OKAY! OKAY! YOU KNOW, YOU COULD'VE JUST ASKED.

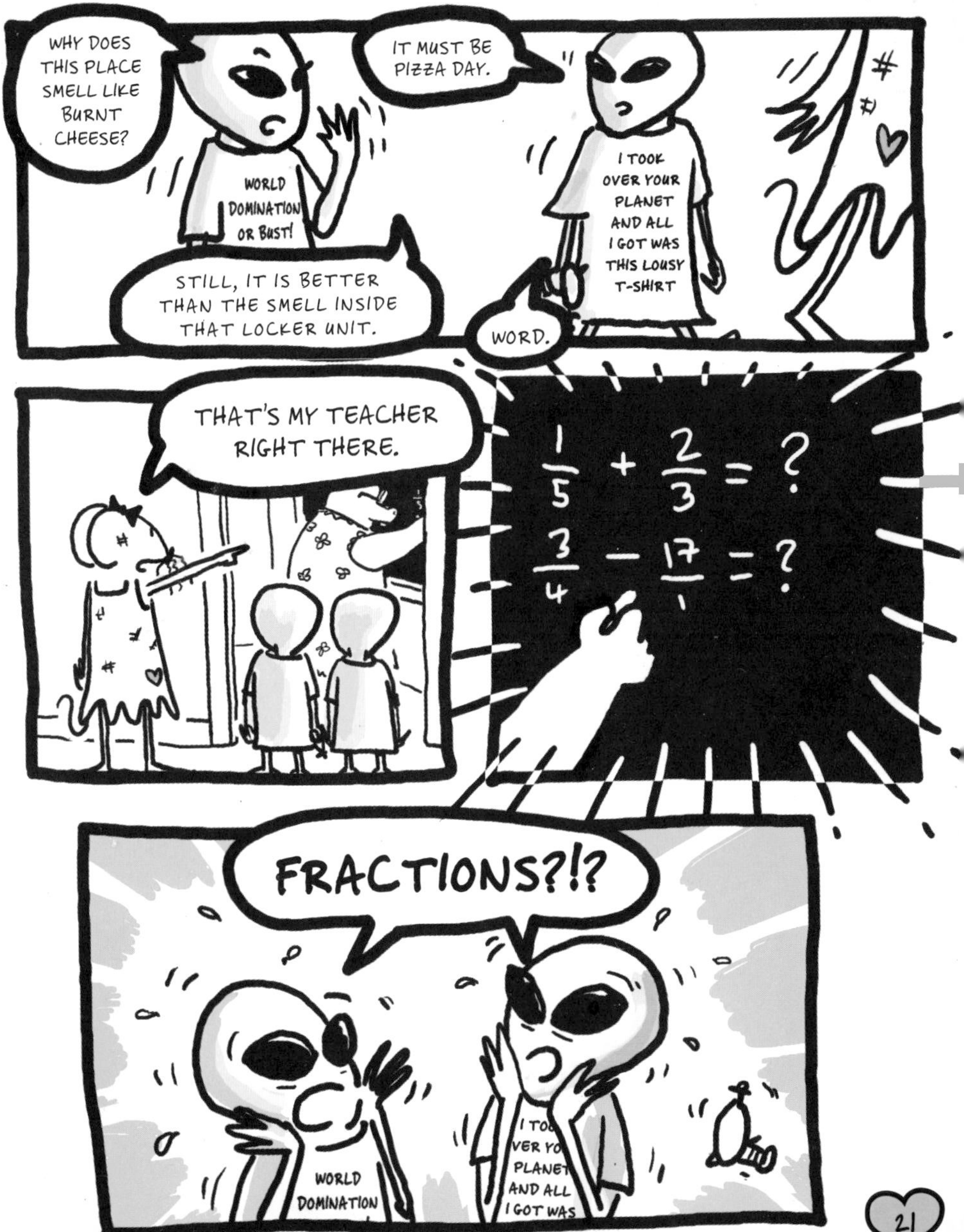
WHY DOES THIS PLACE SMELL LIKE BURNT CHEESE?
WORLD DOMINATION OR BUST!
IT MUST BE PIZZA DAY.
I TOOK OVER YOUR PLANET AND ALL I GOT WAS THIS LOUSY T-SHIRT
STILL, IT IS BETTER THAN THE SMELL INSIDE THAT LOCKER UNIT.
WORD.
THAT'S MY TEACHER RIGHT THERE.
1/5 + 2/3 = ?
3/4 − 17/1 = ?
FRACTIONS?!?
WORLD DOMINATION
I TOO
VER YO
PLANET
AND ALL
I GOT WAS

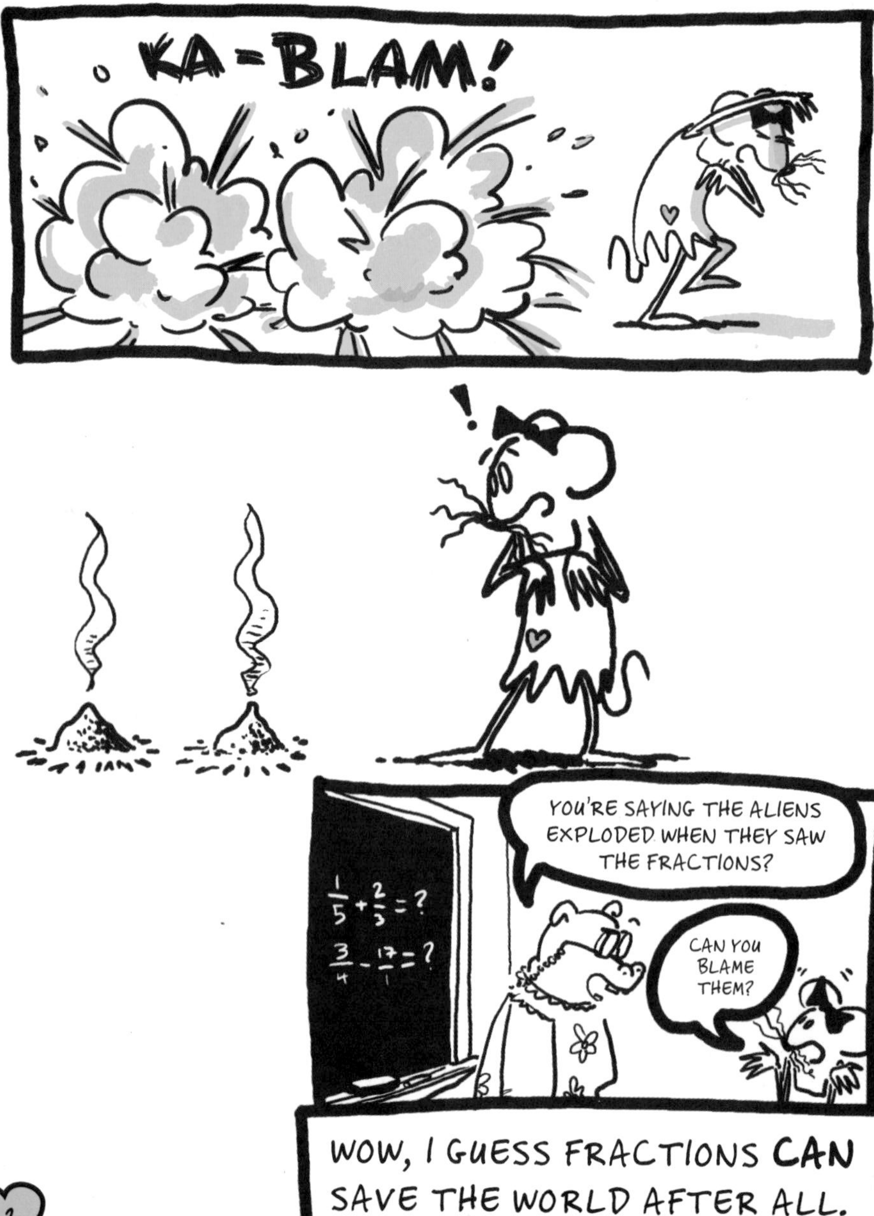
KA-BLAM!
!
YOU'RE SAYING THE ALIENS EXPLODED WHEN THEY SAW THE FRACTIONS?
CAN YOU BLAME THEM?
WOW, I GUESS FRACTIONS CAN SAVE THE WORLD AFTER ALL.

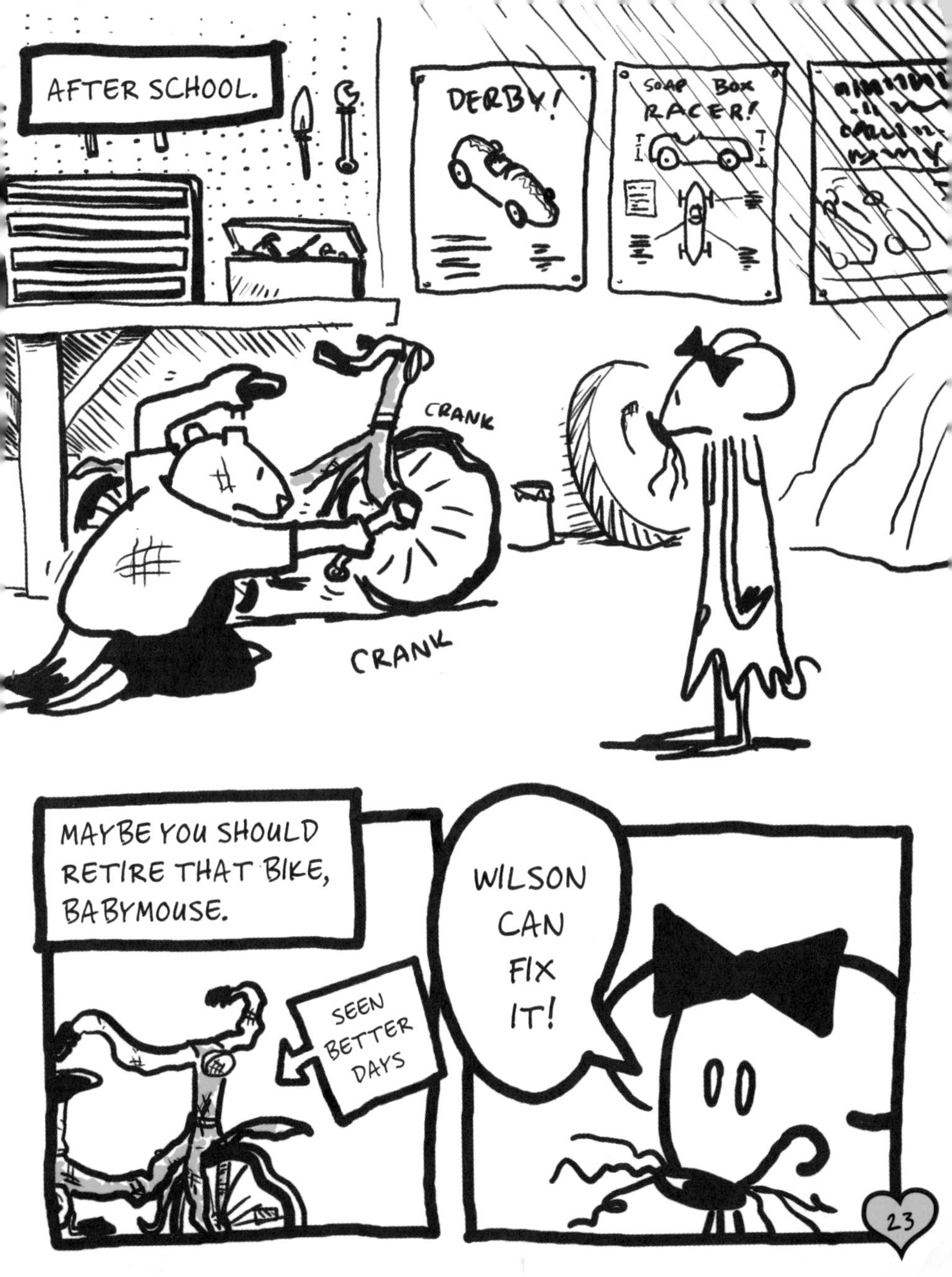
AFTER SCHOOL.
DERBY!
SOAP BOX RACER!
CRANK
CRANK
MAYBE YOU SHOULD RETIRE THAT BIKE, BABYMOUSE.
SEEN BETTER DAYS
WILSON CAN FIX IT!

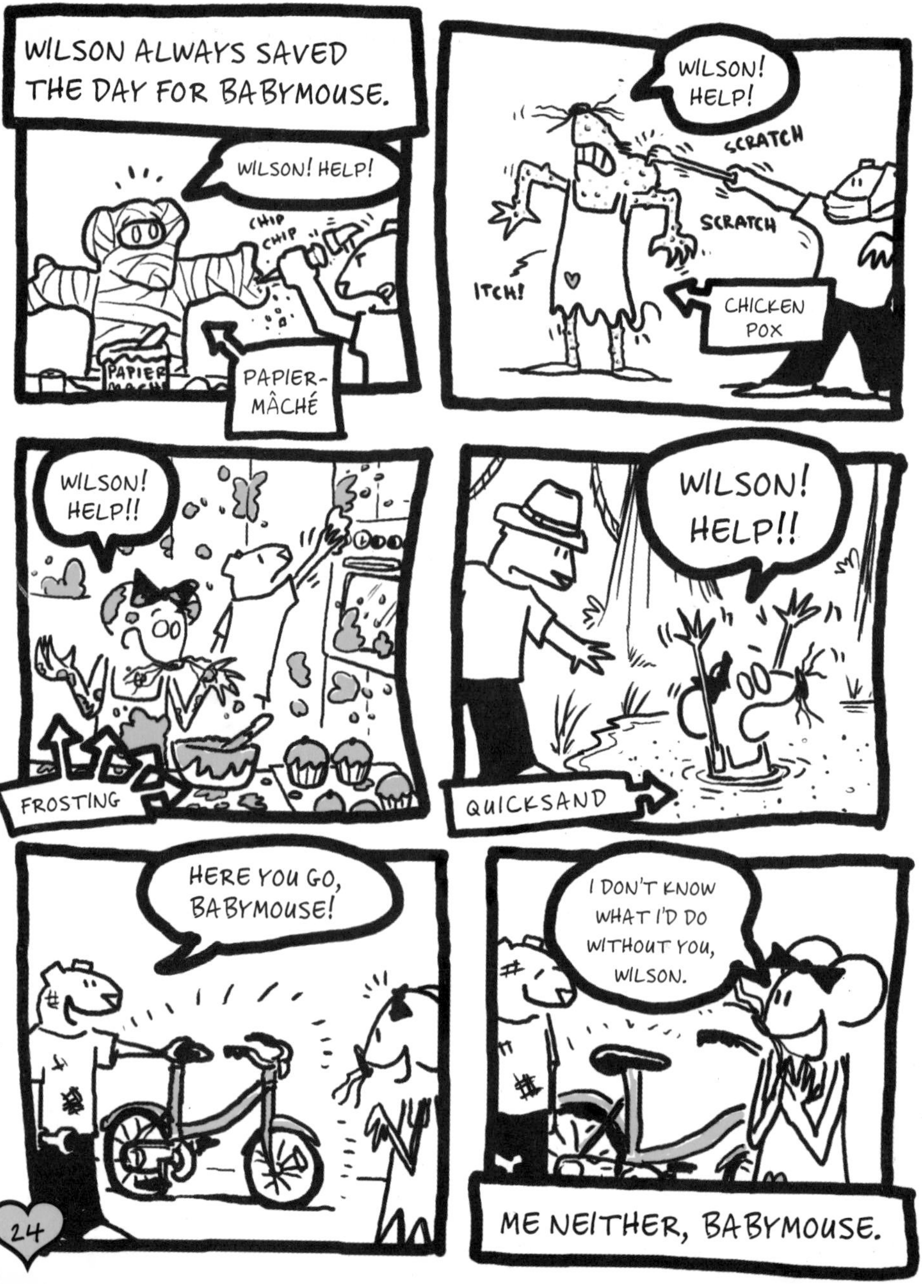
WILSON ALWAYS SAVED THE DAY FOR BABYMOUSE.
WILSON! HELP!
CHIP CHIP
PAPIER
PAPIER-MÂCHÉ
WILSON! HELP!
SCRATCH
SCRATCH
ITCH!
CHICKEN POX
WILSON! HELP!!
FROSTING
WILSON! HELP!!
QUICKSAND
HERE YOU GO, BABYMOUSE!
I DON'T KNOW WHAT I'D DO WITHOUT YOU, WILSON.
ME NEITHER, BABYMOUSE.

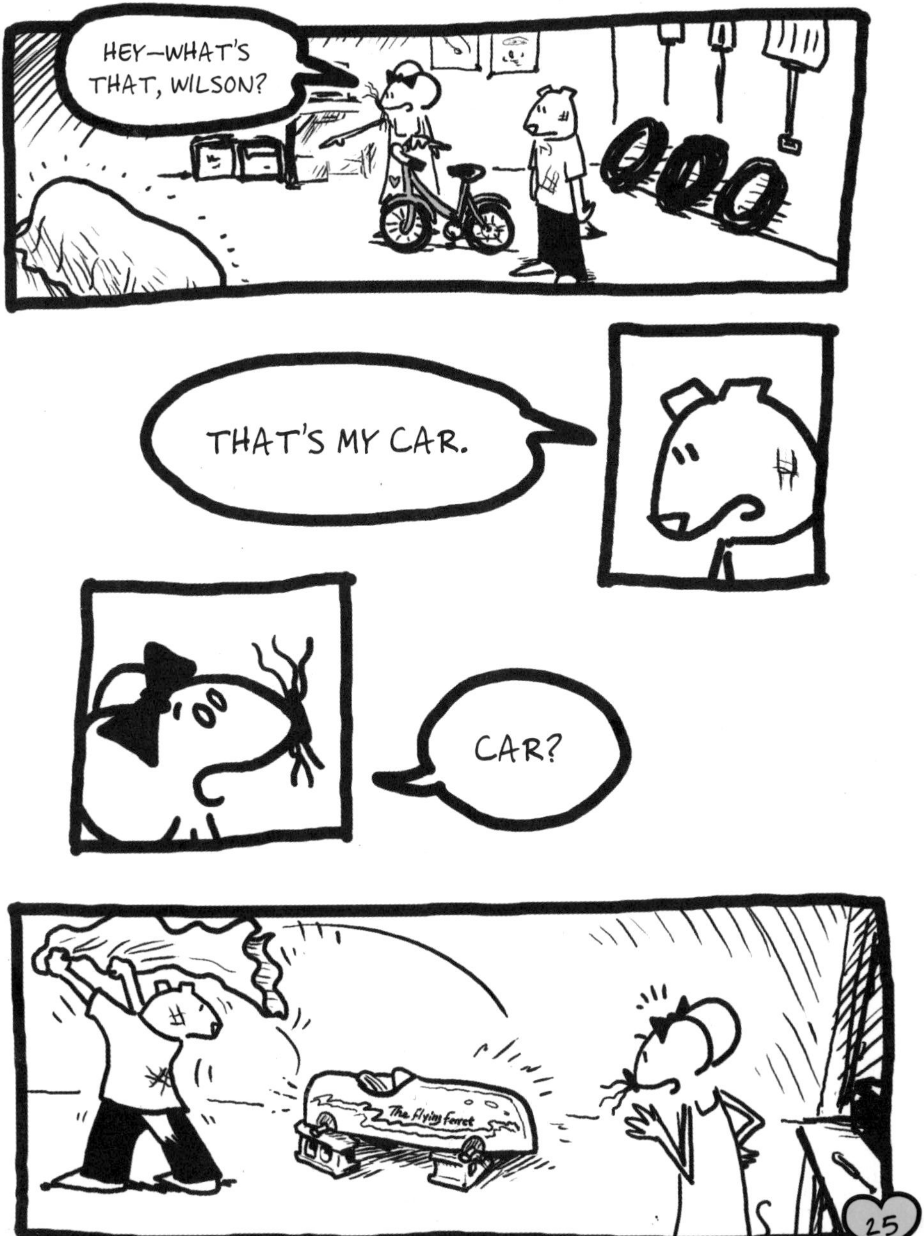
HEY—WHAT'S THAT, WILSON?
THAT'S MY CAR.
CAR?
The Flying Ferret

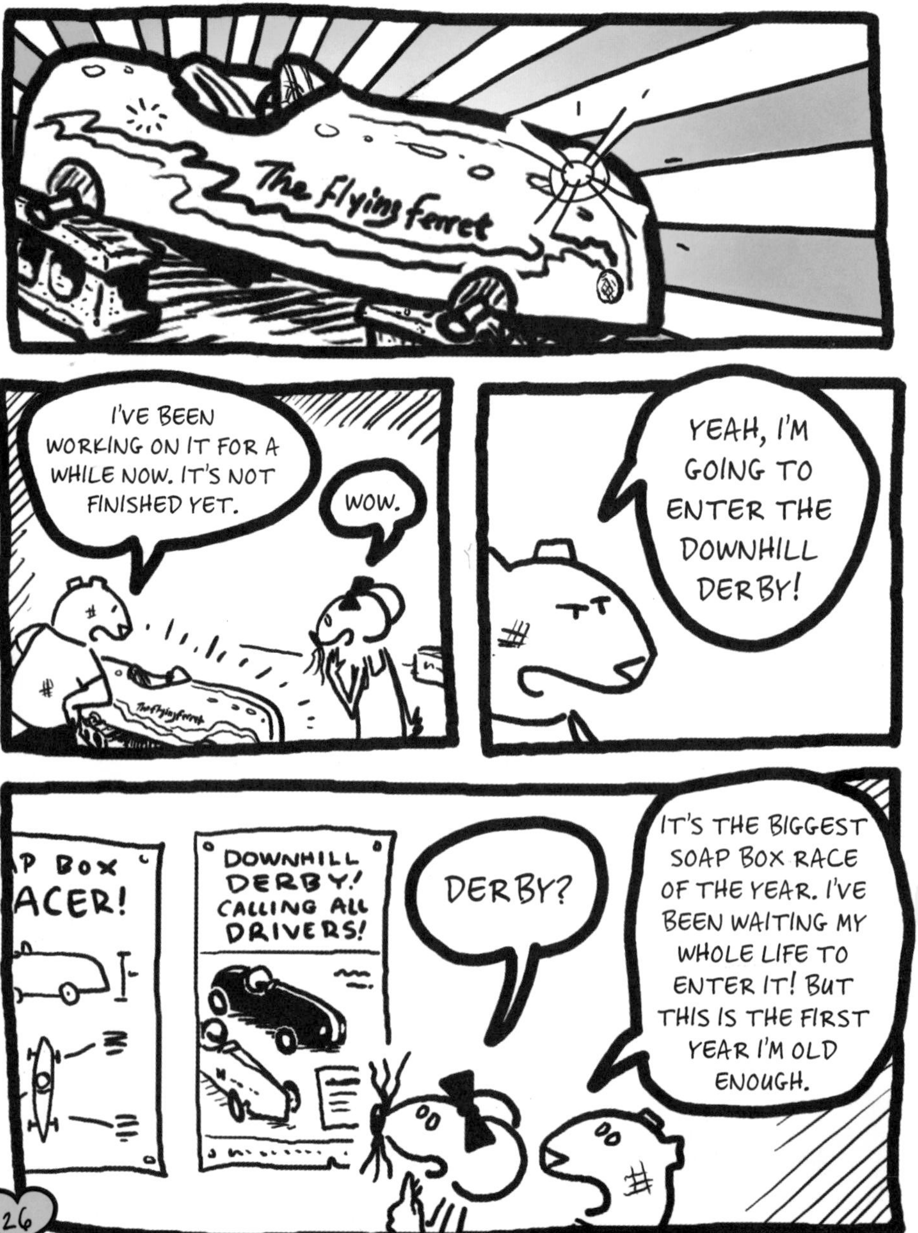
The Flying Ferret
I'VE BEEN WORKING ON IT FOR A WHILE NOW. IT'S NOT FINISHED YET.
WOW.
YEAH, I'M GOING TO ENTER THE DOWNHILL DERBY!
DOWNHILL DERBY! CALLING ALL DRIVERS!
DERBY?
IT'S THE BIGGEST SOAP BOX RACE OF THE YEAR. I'VE BEEN WAITING MY WHOLE LIFE TO ENTER IT! BUT THIS IS THE FIRST YEAR I'M OLD ENOUGH.

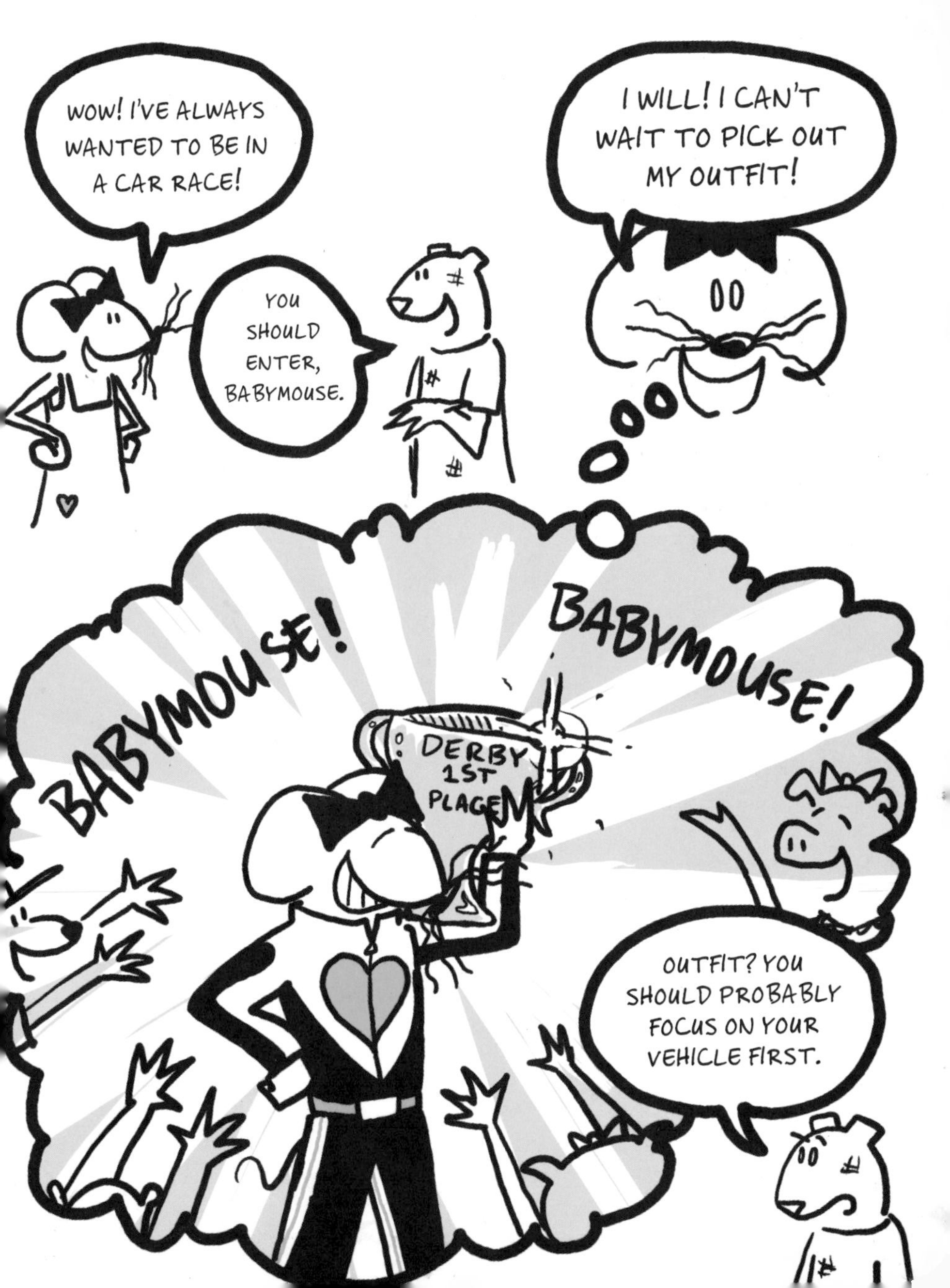
WOW! I'VE ALWAYS WANTED TO BE IN A CAR RACE!
YOU SHOULD ENTER, BABYMOUSE.
I WILL! I CAN'T WAIT TO PICK OUT MY OUTFIT!
BABYMOUSE!
BABYMOUSE!
DERBY 1ST PLACE
OUTFIT? YOU SHOULD PROBABLY FOCUS ON YOUR VEHICLE FIRST.

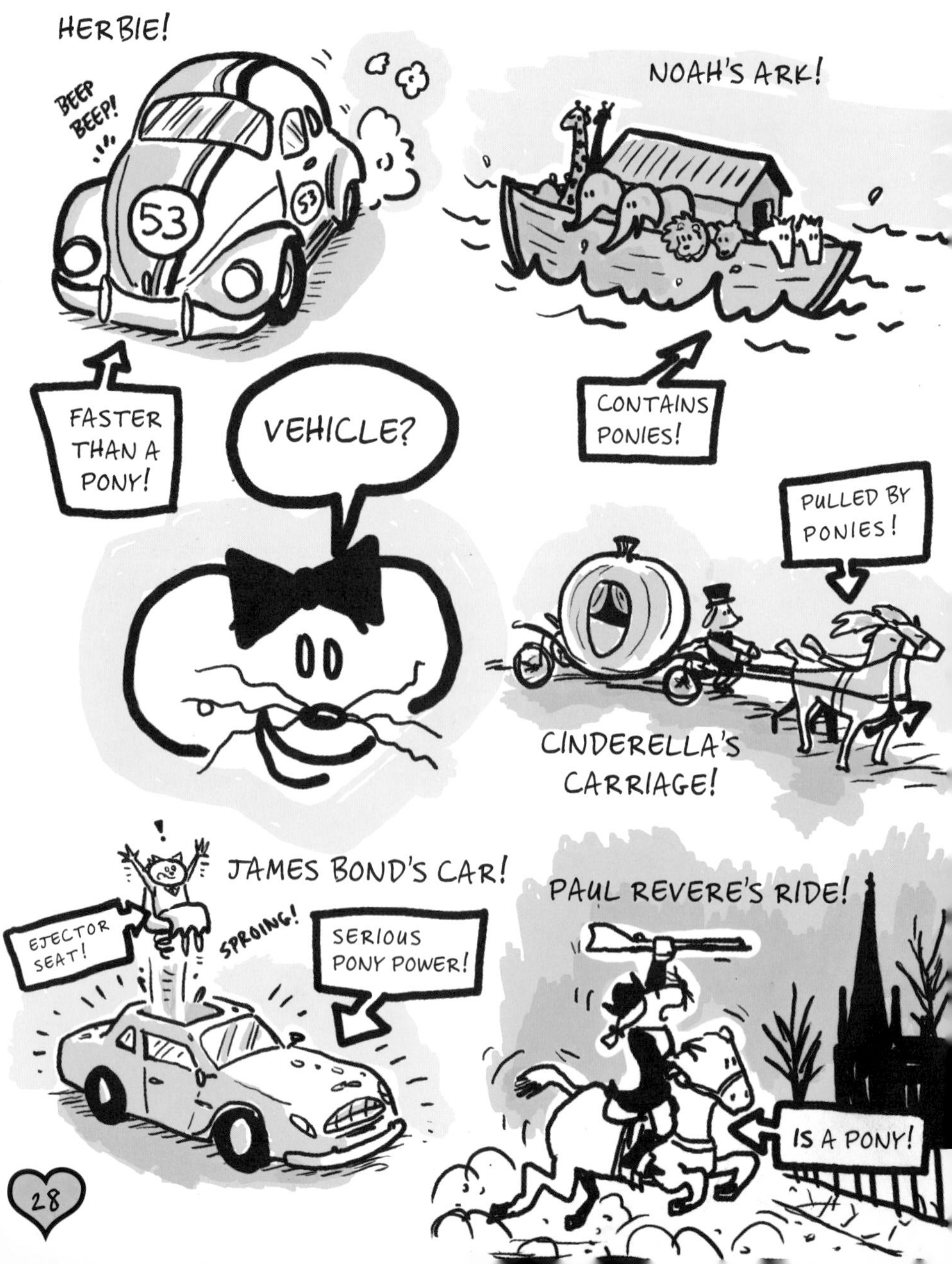
HERBIE!
BEEP BEEP!
53
53
FASTER THAN A PONY!
NOAH'S ARK!
CONTAINS PONIES!
VEHICLE?
PULLED BY PONIES!
CINDERELLA'S CARRIAGE!
JAMES BOND'S CAR!
EJECTOR SEAT!
SPROING!
SERIOUS PONY POWER!
PAUL REVERE'S RIDE!
IS A PONY!
28

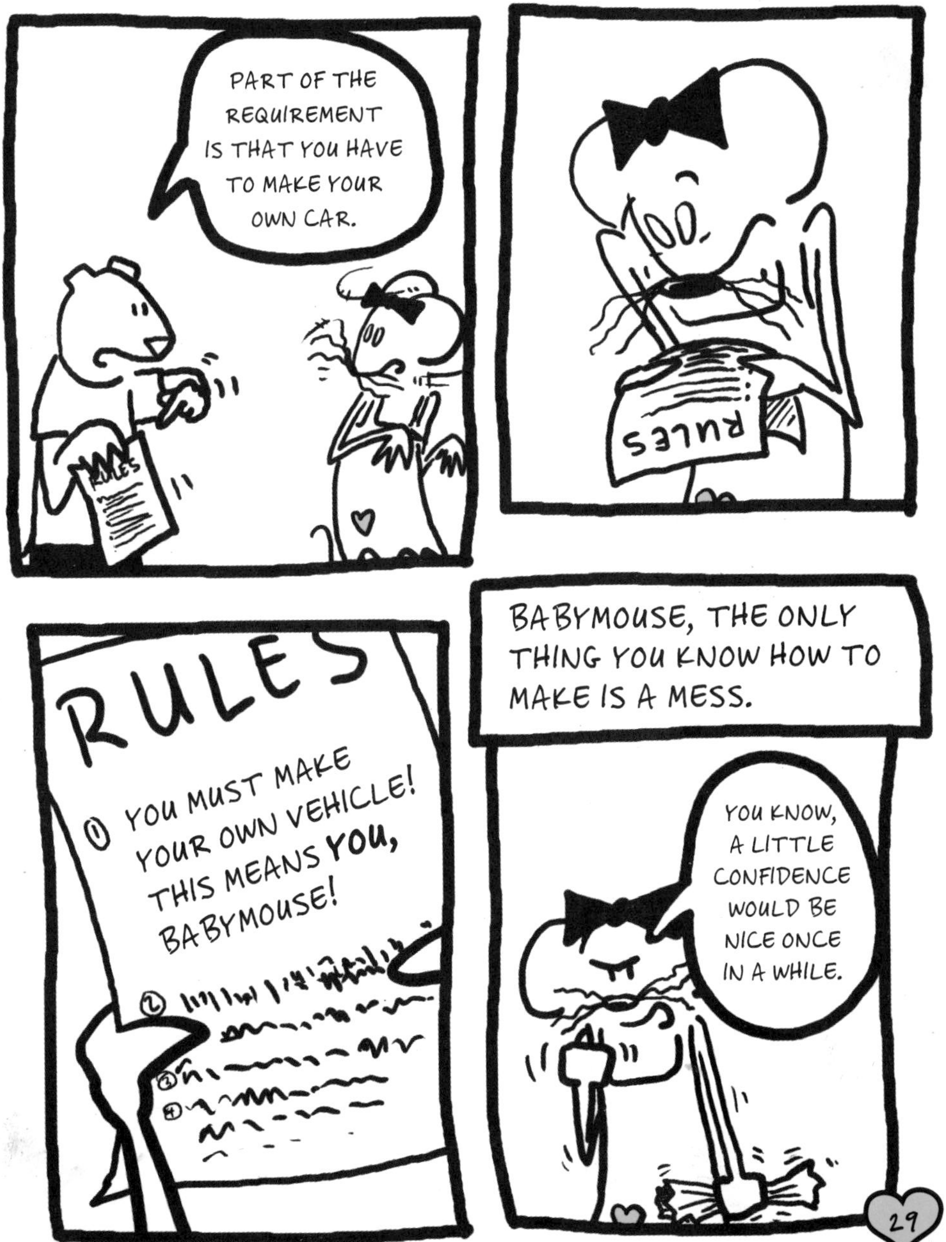
PART OF THE REQUIREMENT IS THAT YOU HAVE TO MAKE YOUR OWN CAR.
RULES
RULES
RULES
① YOU MUST MAKE YOUR OWN VEHICLE! THIS MEANS **YOU**, BABYMOUSE!
BABYMOUSE, THE ONLY THING YOU KNOW HOW TO MAKE IS A MESS.
YOU KNOW, A LITTLE CONFIDENCE WOULD BE NICE ONCE IN A WHILE.

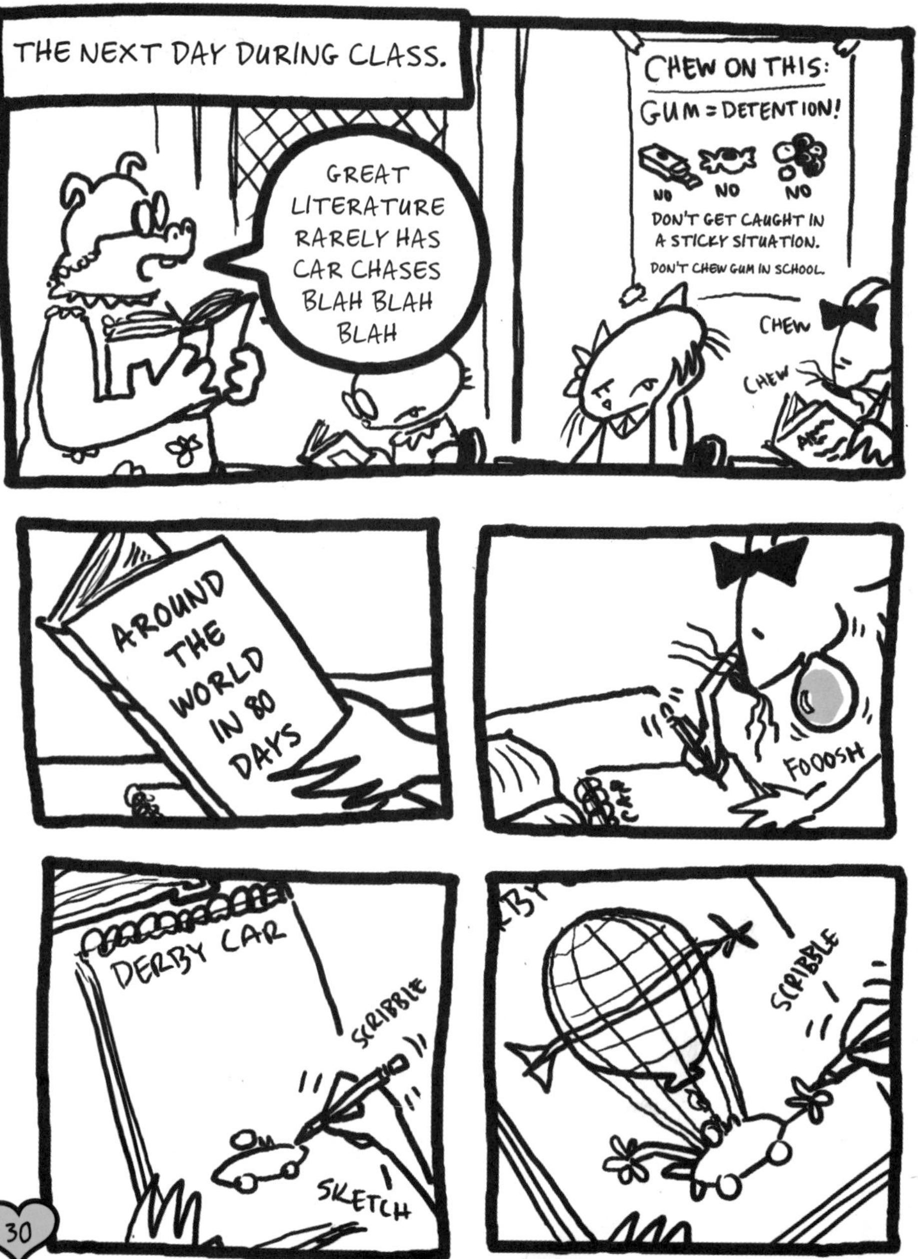
THE NEXT DAY DURING CLASS.
GREAT LITERATURE RARELY HAS CAR CHASES BLAH BLAH BLAH
CHEW ON THIS:
GUM = DETENTION!
NO
NO
NO
DON'T GET CAUGHT IN A STICKY SITUATION.
DON'T CHEW GUM IN SCHOOL.
CHEW
CHEW
AROUND THE WORLD IN 80 DAYS
FOOOSH
DERBY CAR
SCRIBBLE
SKETCH
SCRIBBLE

AROUND THE SCHOOL

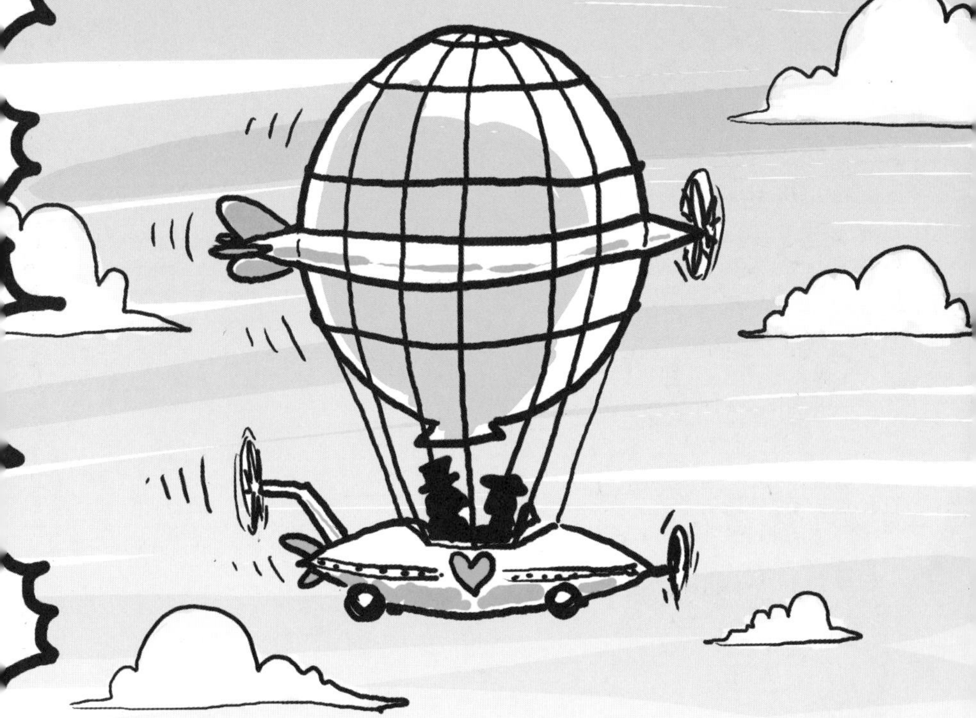

IN 8 PERIODS!

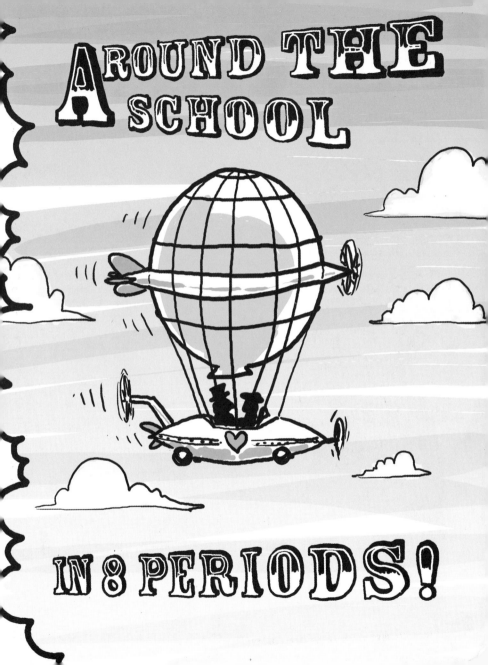

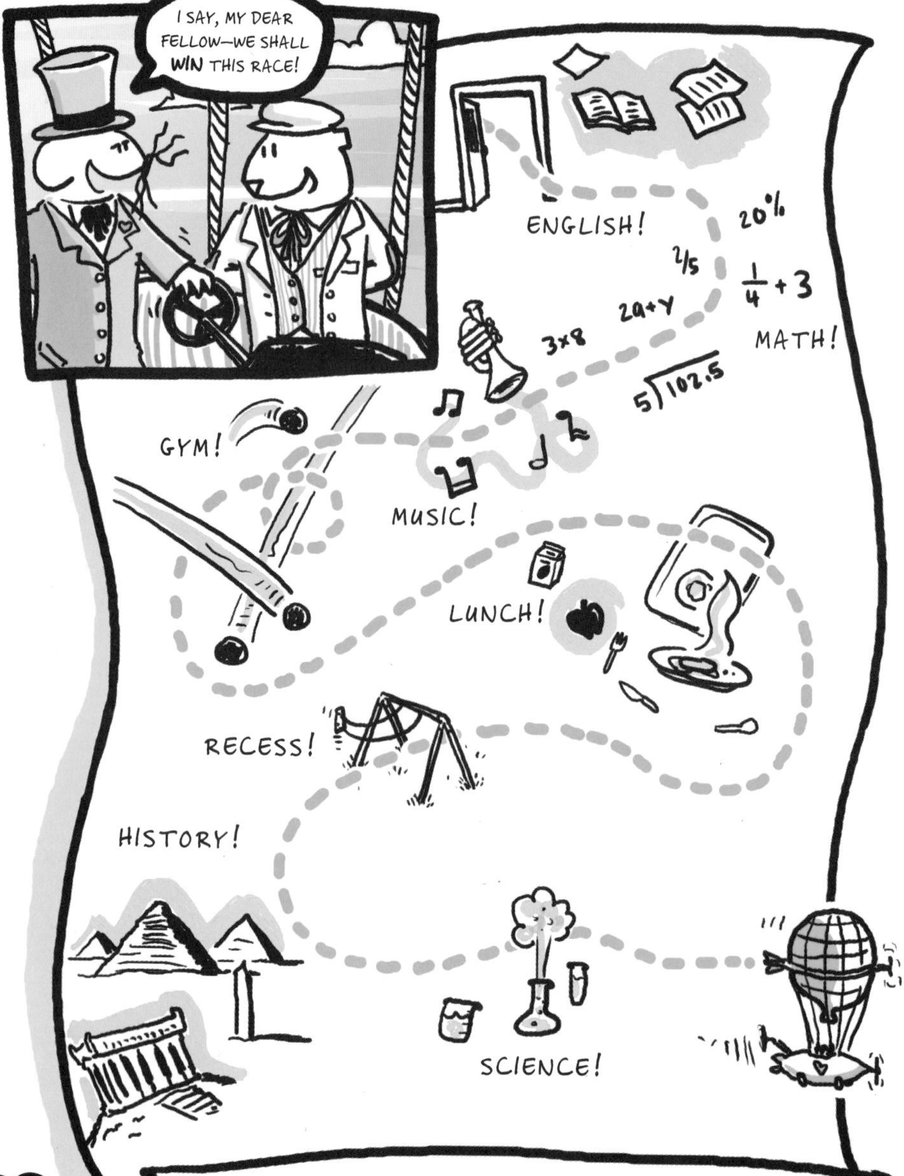
I SAY, MY DEAR FELLOW—WE SHALL **WIN** THIS RACE!
ENGLISH!
20%
2/5
1/4 + 3
2a+Y
3×8
MATH!
5)102.5
GYM!
MUSIC!
LUNCH!
RECESS!
HISTORY!
SCIENCE!

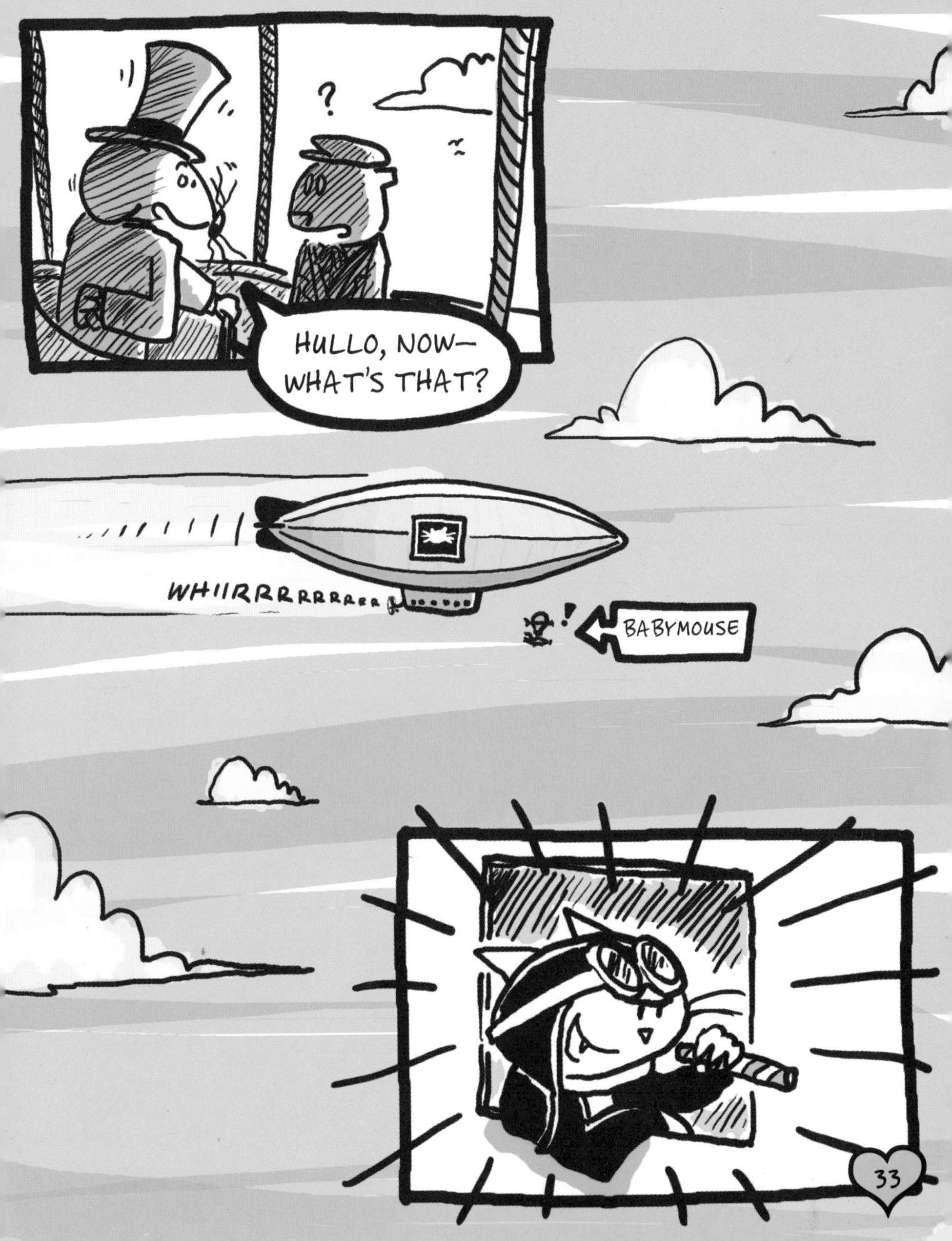
?
HULLO, NOW—
WHAT'S THAT?
WHIIRRRRRRRRRR
BABYMOUSE

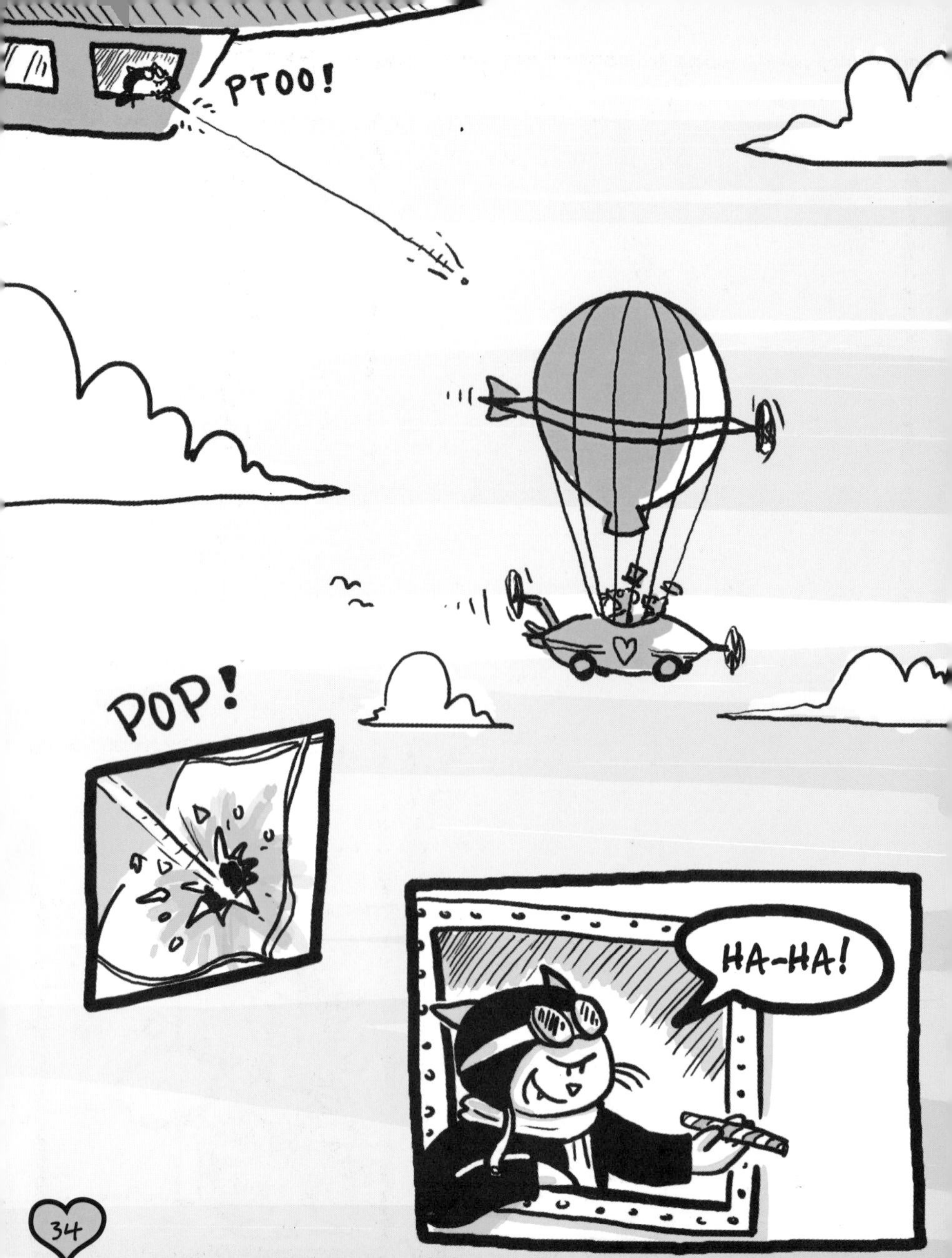
PTOO!
POP!
HA-HA!

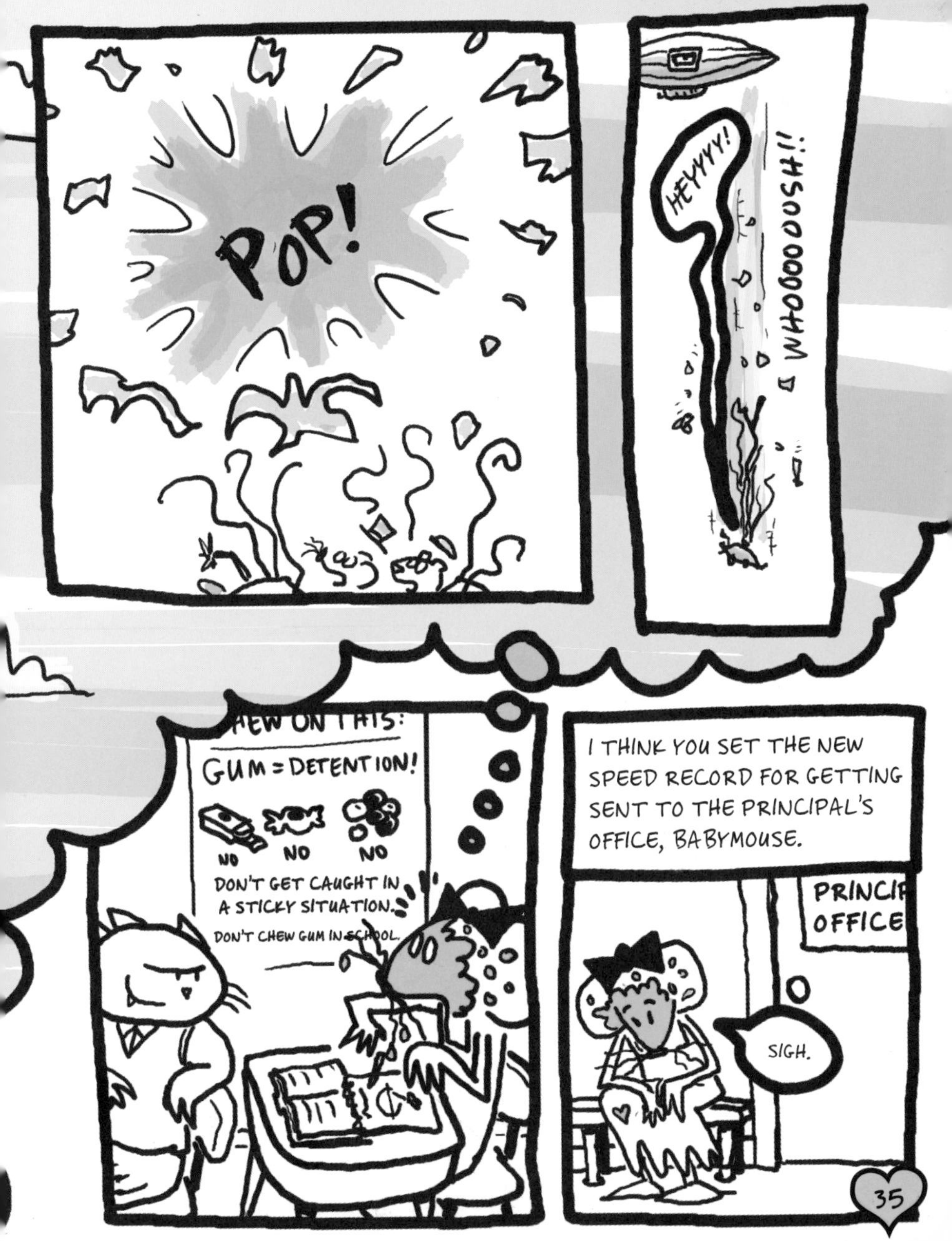
POP!
HEYYYY!
WHOOOOOOSH!!
CHEW ON THIS:
GUM = DETENTION!
NO NO NO
DON'T GET CAUGHT IN A STICKY SITUATION.
DON'T CHEW GUM IN SCHOOL.
I THINK YOU SET THE NEW SPEED RECORD FOR GETTING SENT TO THE PRINCIPAL'S OFFICE, BABYMOUSE.
PRINCI
OFFICE
SIGH.

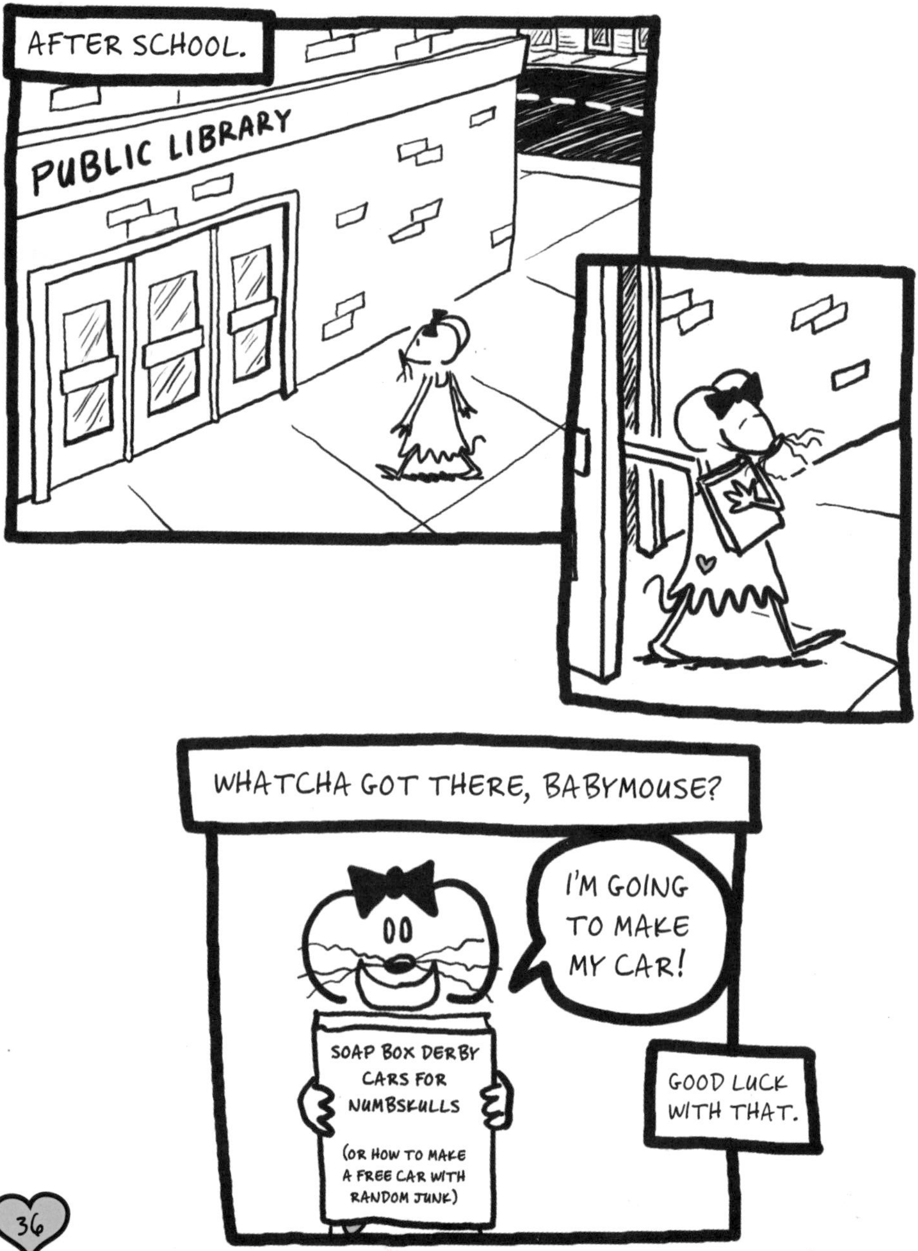

AFTER SCHOOL.
PUBLIC LIBRARY
WHATCHA GOT THERE, BABYMOUSE?
I'M GOING TO MAKE MY CAR!
SOAP BOX DERBY CARS FOR NUMBSKULLS
(OR HOW TO MAKE A FREE CAR WITH RANDOM JUNK)
GOOD LUCK WITH THAT.

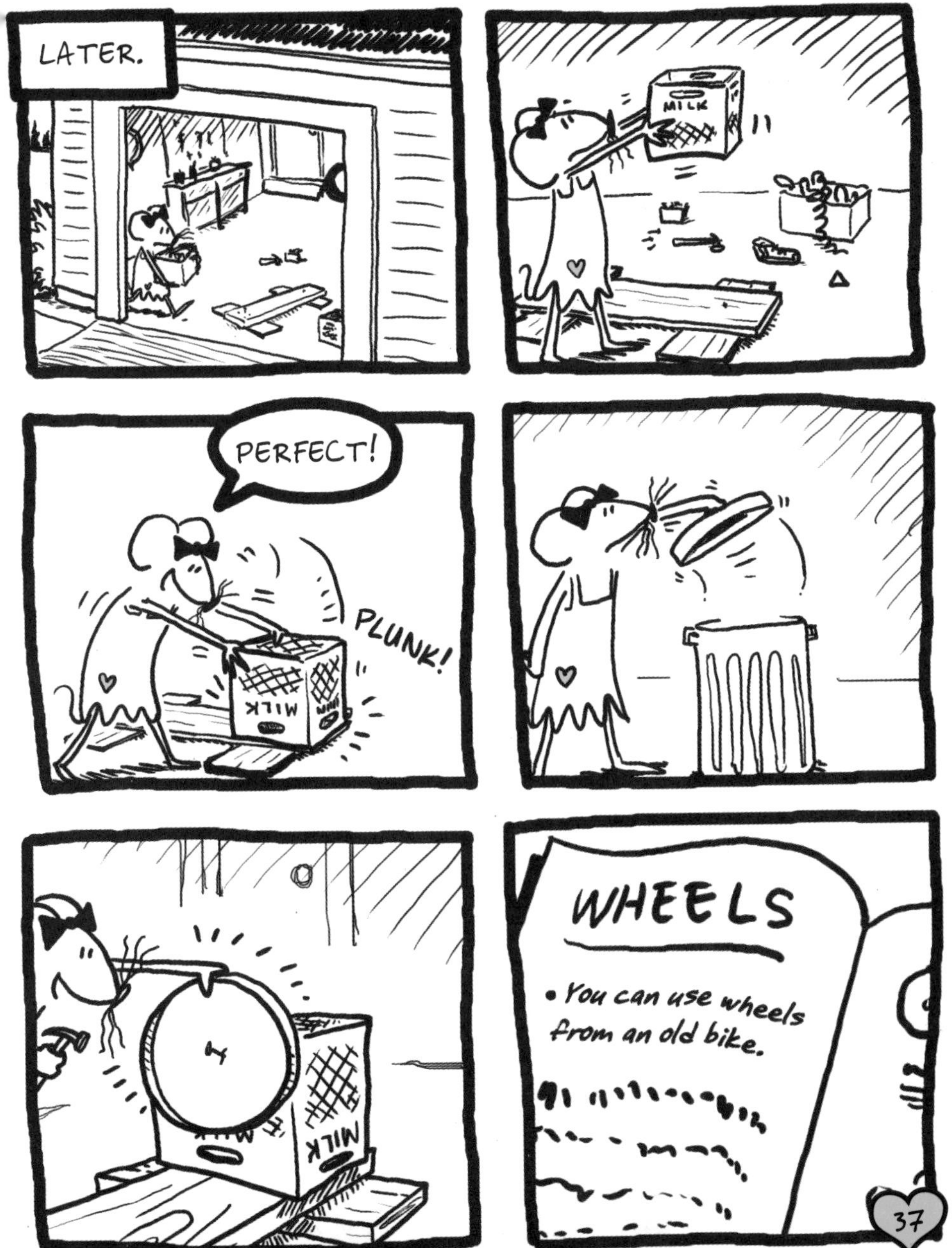
LATER.
PERFECT!
PLUNK!
WHEELS
• You can use wheels from an old bike.

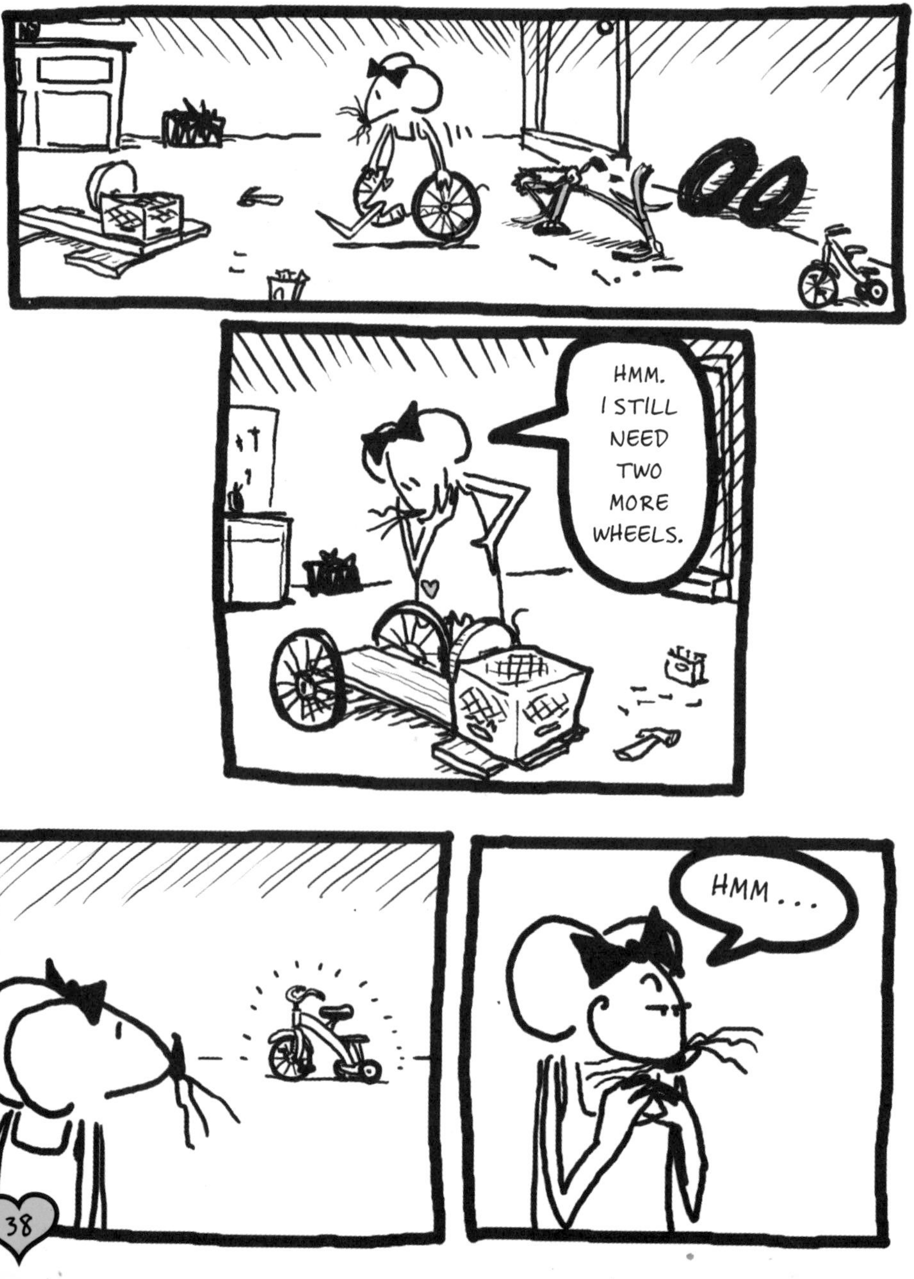
HMM. I STILL NEED TWO MORE WHEELS.
HMM . . .

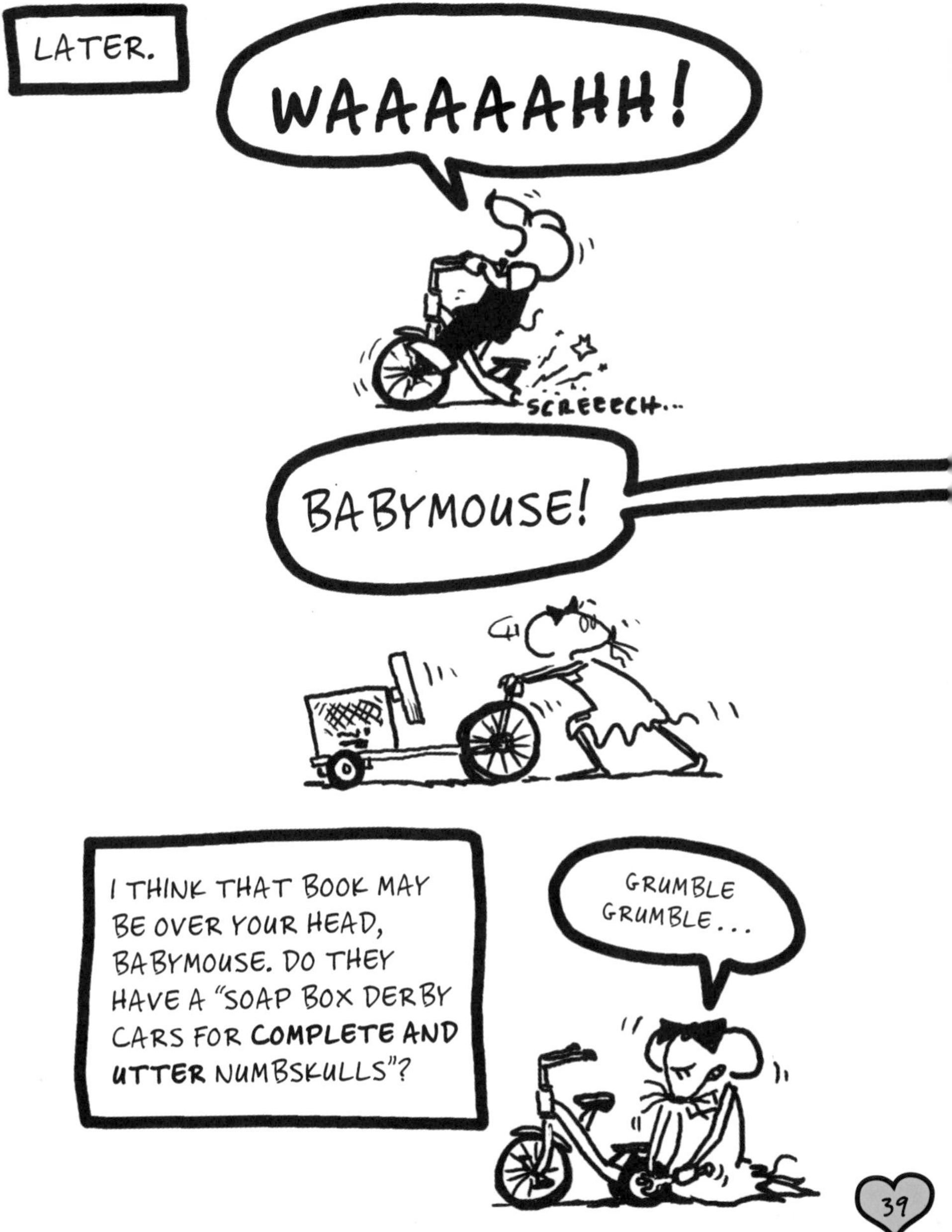
LATER.
WAAAAAHH!
SCREEECH...
BABYMOUSE!
I THINK THAT BOOK MAY BE OVER YOUR HEAD, BABYMOUSE. DO THEY HAVE A "SOAP BOX DERBY CARS FOR **COMPLETE AND UTTER** NUMBSKULLS"?
GRUMBLE GRUMBLE...

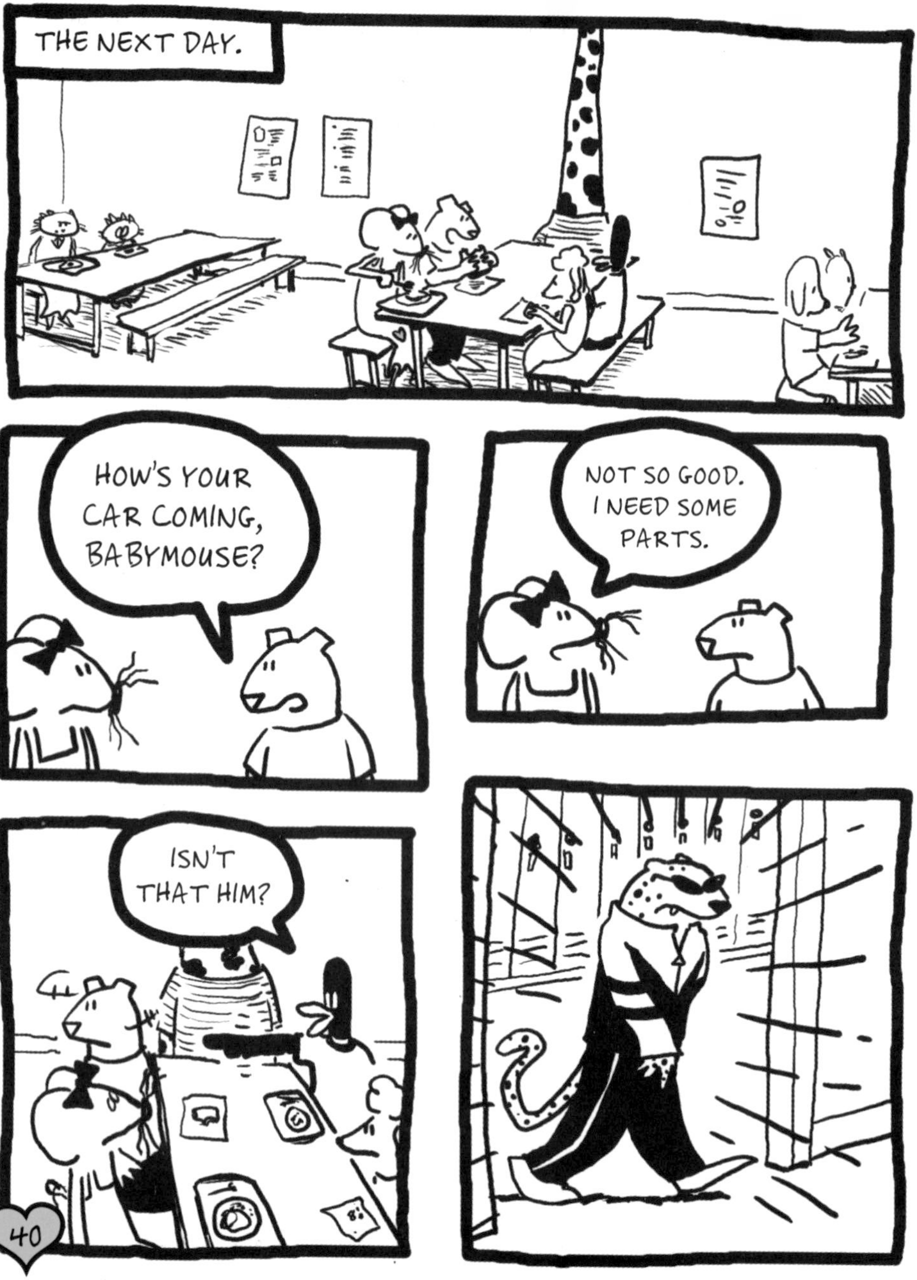
THE NEXT DAY.
HOW'S YOUR CAR COMING, BABYMOUSE?
NOT SO GOOD. I NEED SOME PARTS.
ISN'T THAT HIM?

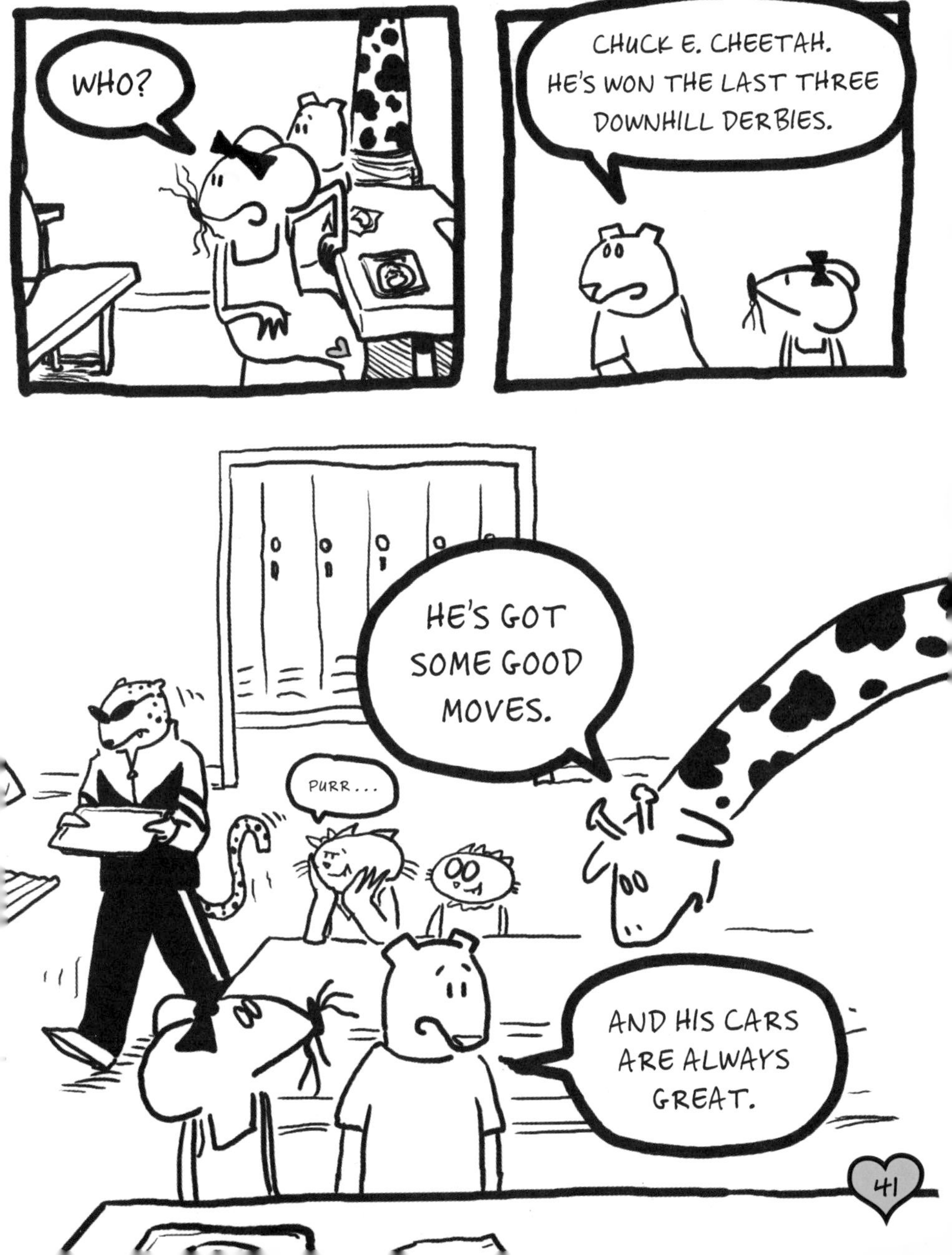
WHO?
CHUCK E. CHEETAH. HE'S WON THE LAST THREE DOWNHILL DERBIES.
HE'S GOT SOME GOOD MOVES.
PURR...
AND HIS CARS ARE ALWAYS GREAT.

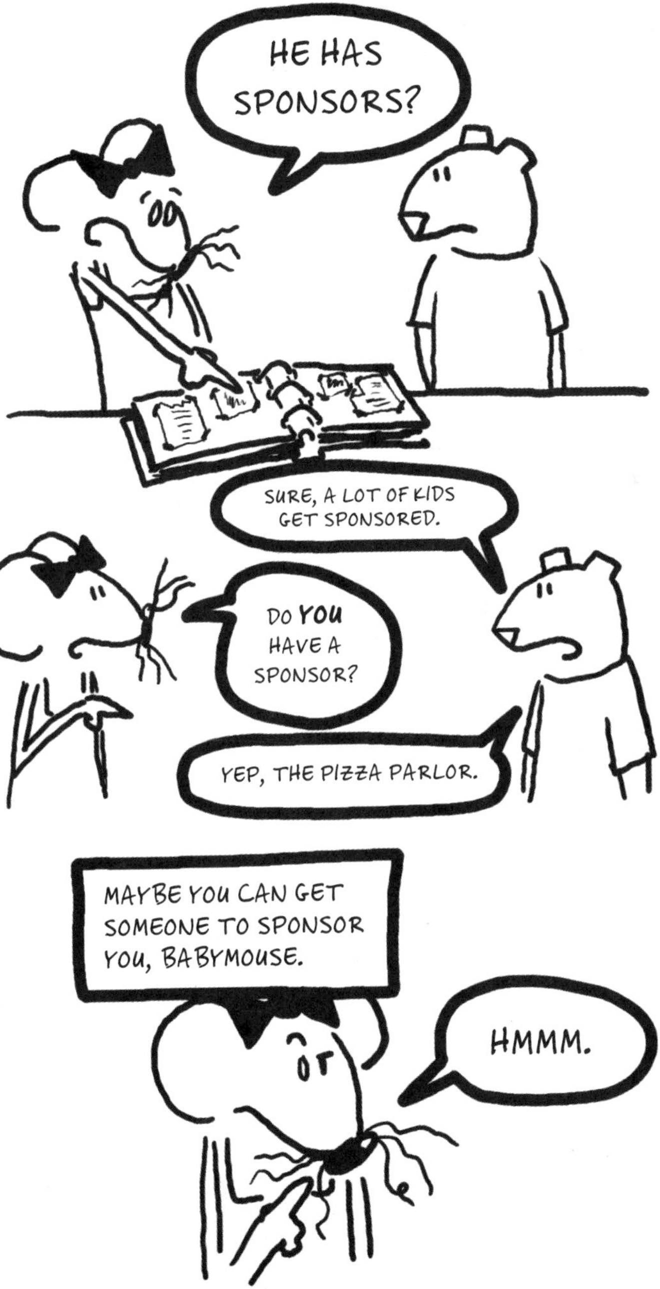
HE HAS SPONSORS?
SURE, A LOT OF KIDS GET SPONSORED.
DO **YOU** HAVE A SPONSOR?
YEP, THE PIZZA PARLOR.
MAYBE YOU CAN GET SOMEONE TO SPONSOR YOU, BABYMOUSE.
HMMM.

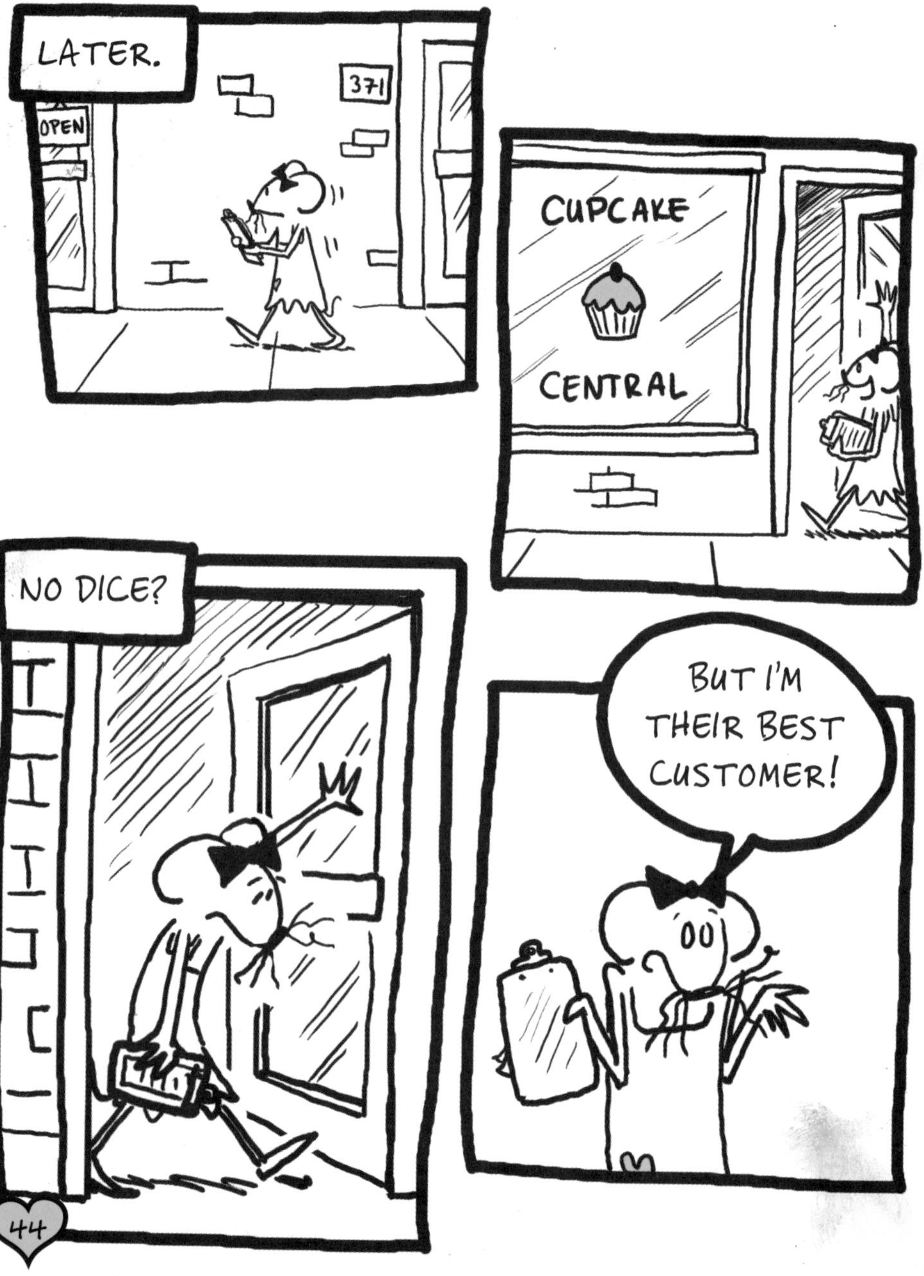
LATER.
OPEN
371
CUPCAKE
CENTRAL
NO DICE?
BUT I'M THEIR BEST CUSTOMER!

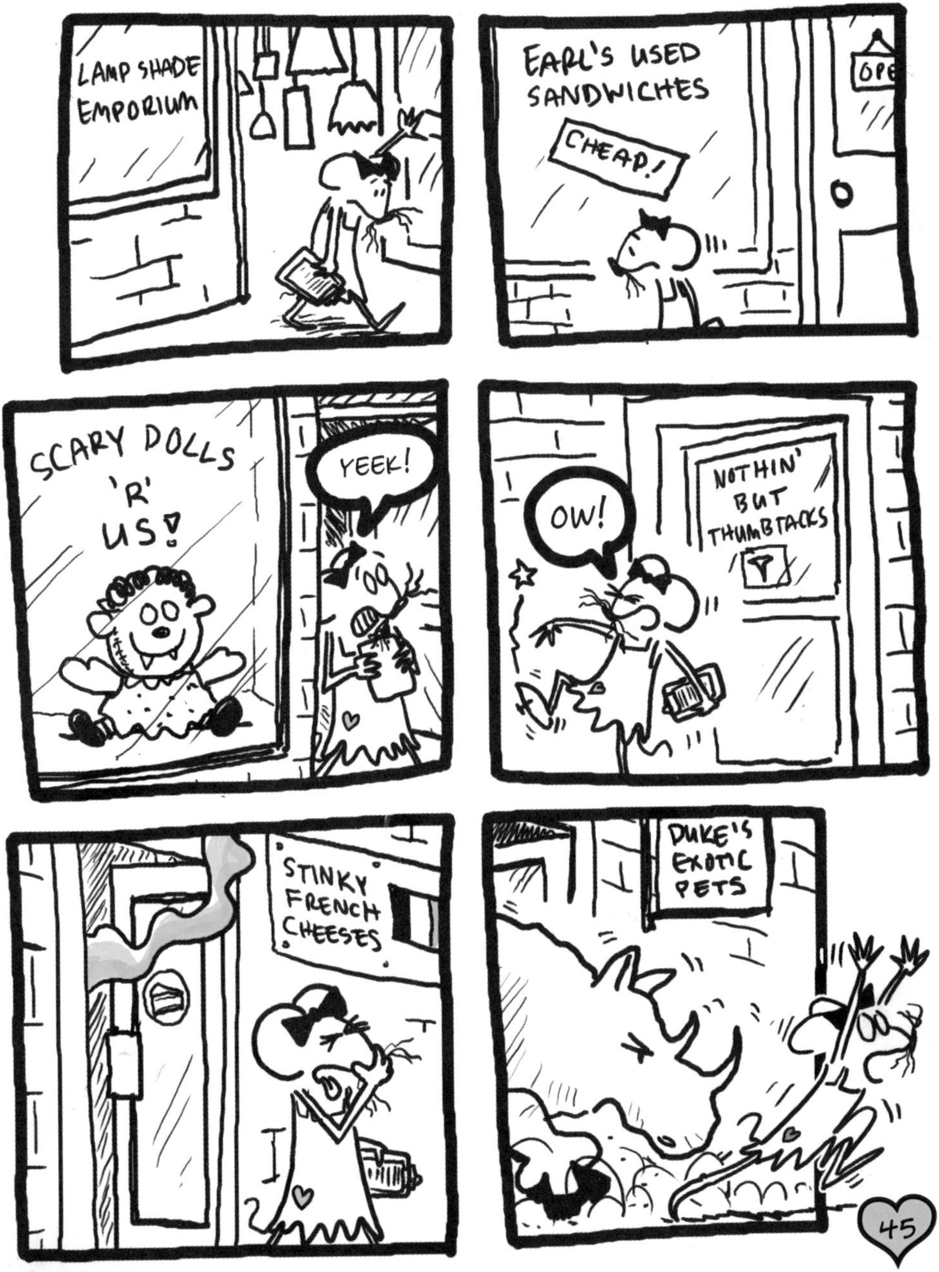
LAMP SHADE EMPORIUM
EARL'S USED SANDWICHES
CHEAP!
OPE
SCARY DOLLS 'R' US!
YEEK!
OW!
NOTHIN' BUT THUMBTACKS
STINKY FRENCH CHEESES
DUKE'S EXOTIC PETS

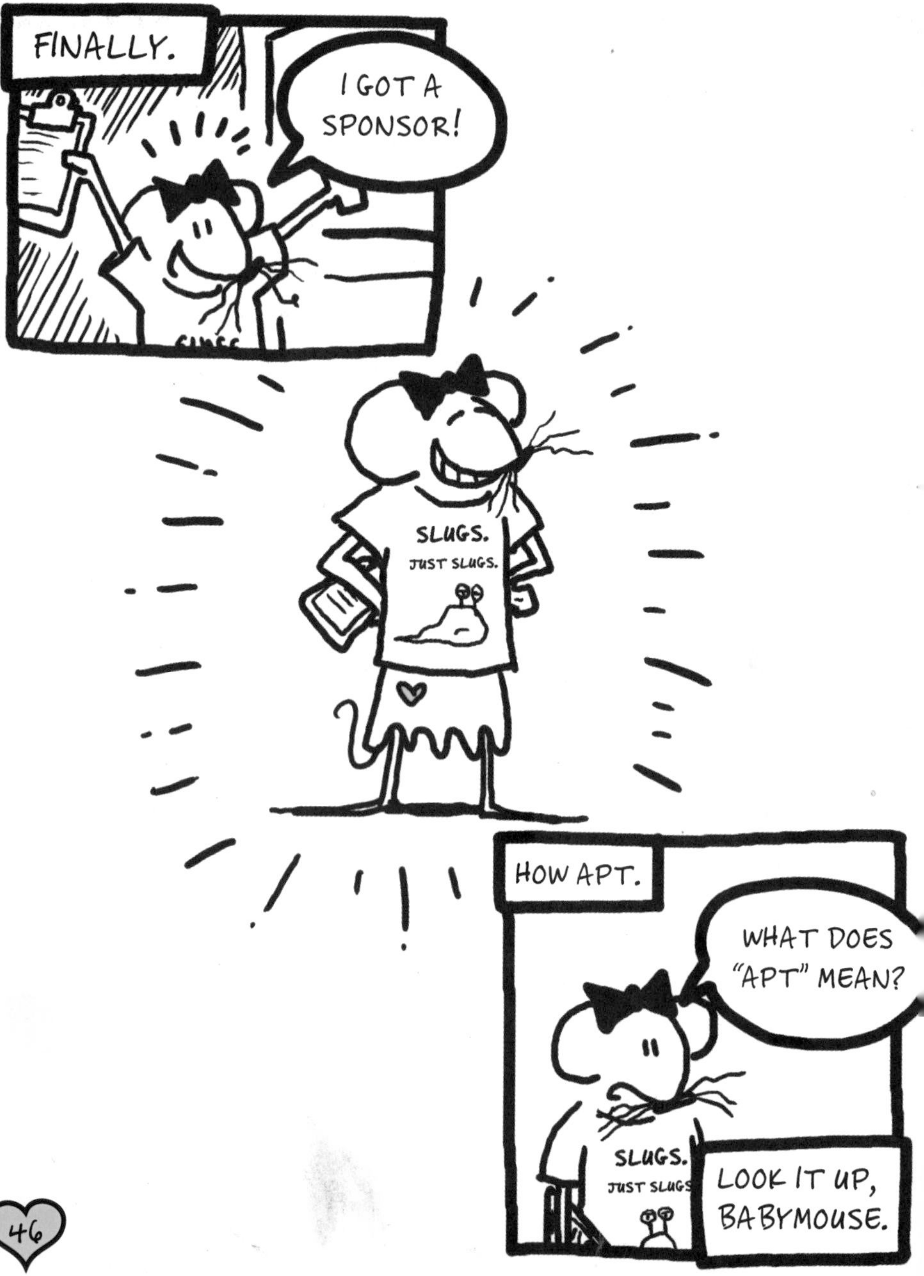
FINALLY.
I GOT A SPONSOR!
SLUGS.
JUST SLUGS.
HOW APT.
WHAT DOES "APT" MEAN?
SLUGS.
JUST SLUGS
LOOK IT UP, BABYMOUSE.

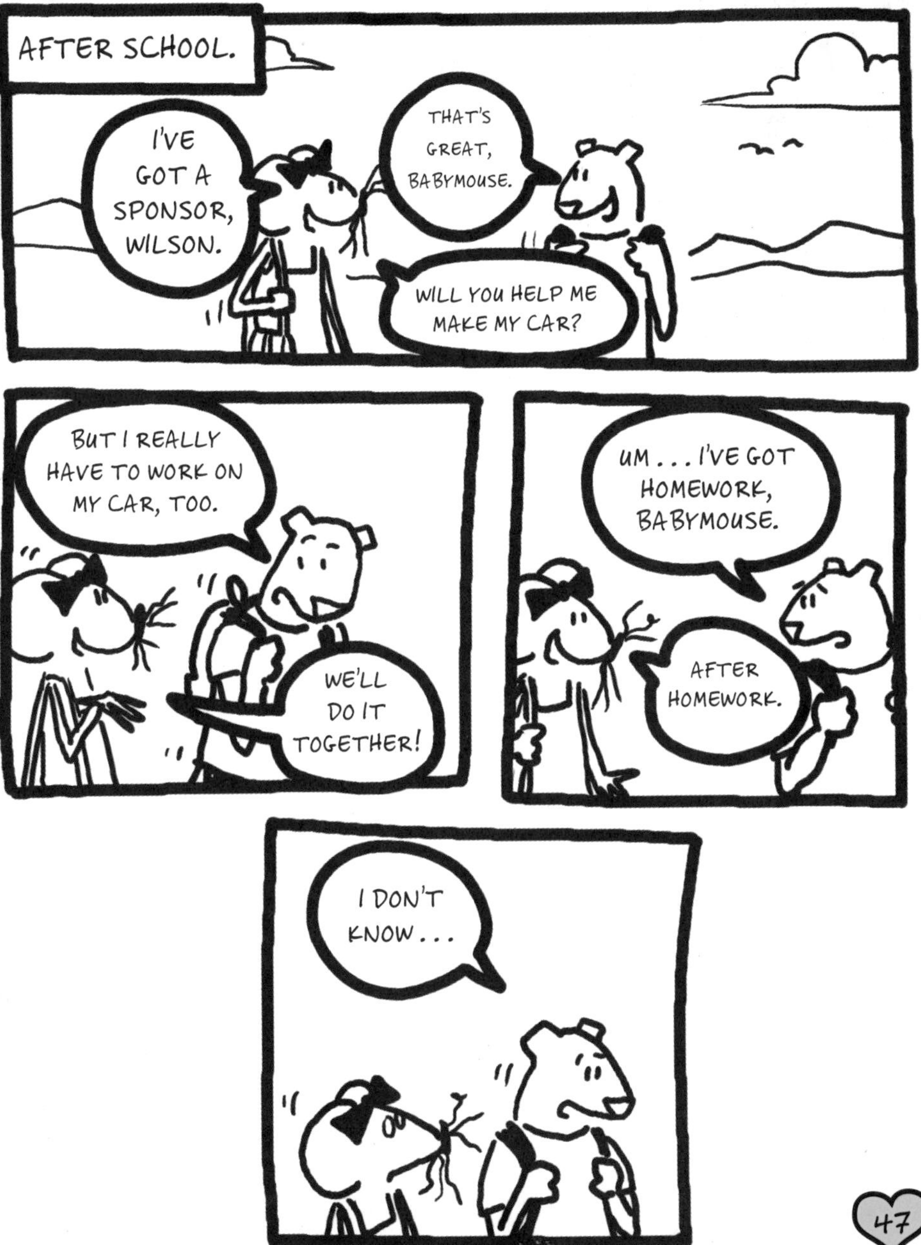
AFTER SCHOOL.
I'VE GOT A SPONSOR, WILSON.
THAT'S GREAT, BABYMOUSE.
WILL YOU HELP ME MAKE MY CAR?
BUT I REALLY HAVE TO WORK ON MY CAR, TOO.
WE'LL DO IT TOGETHER!
UM . . . I'VE GOT HOMEWORK, BABYMOUSE.
AFTER HOMEWORK.
I DON'T KNOW . . .

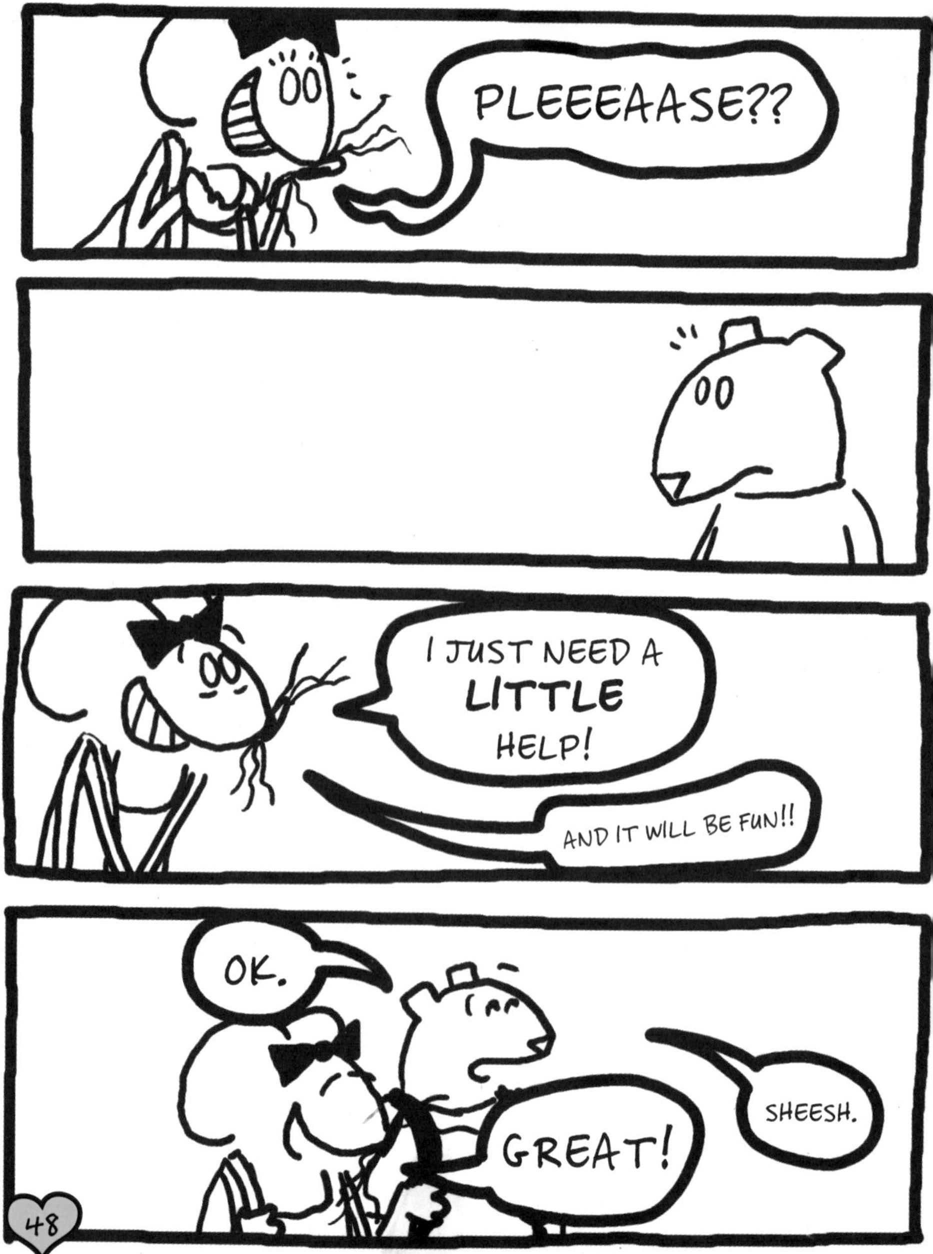
PLEEEAASE??
I JUST NEED A LITTLE HELP!
AND IT WILL BE FUN!!
OK.
GREAT!
SHEESH.

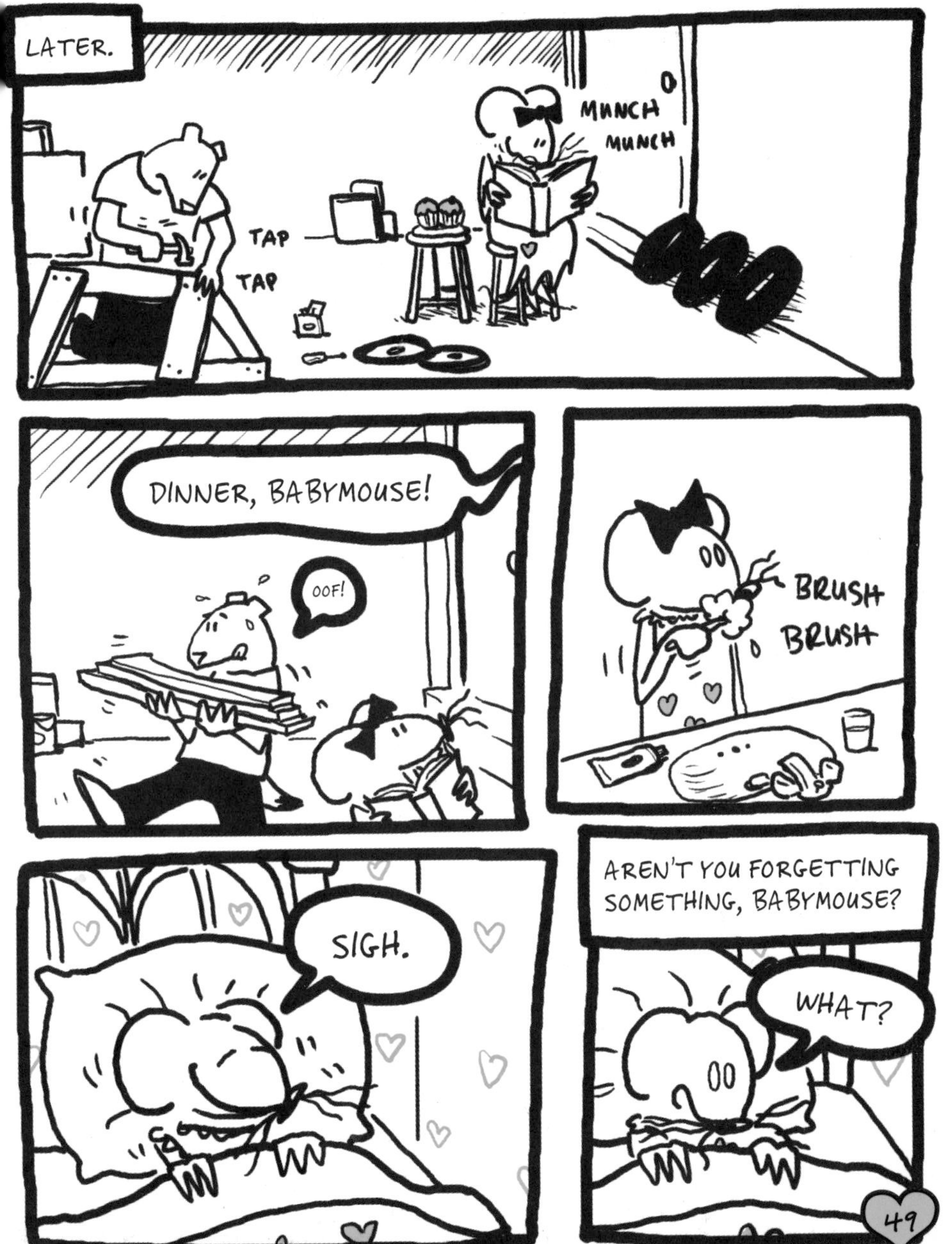
LATER.
TAP
TAP
MUNCH
MUNCH
DINNER, BABYMOUSE!
OOF!
BRUSH
BRUSH
SIGH.
AREN'T YOU FORGETTING SOMETHING, BABYMOUSE?
WHAT?

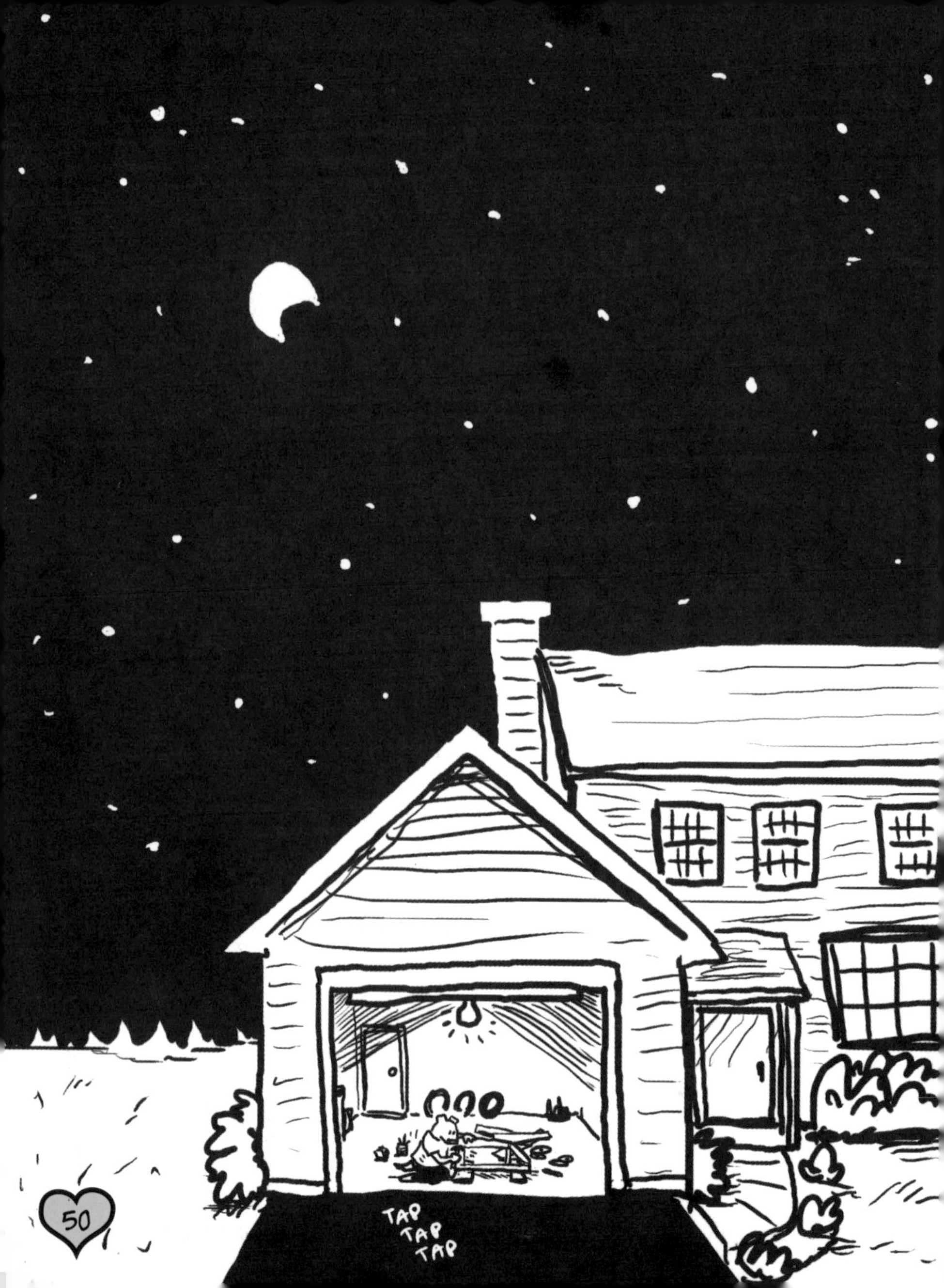
TAP
TAP
TAP

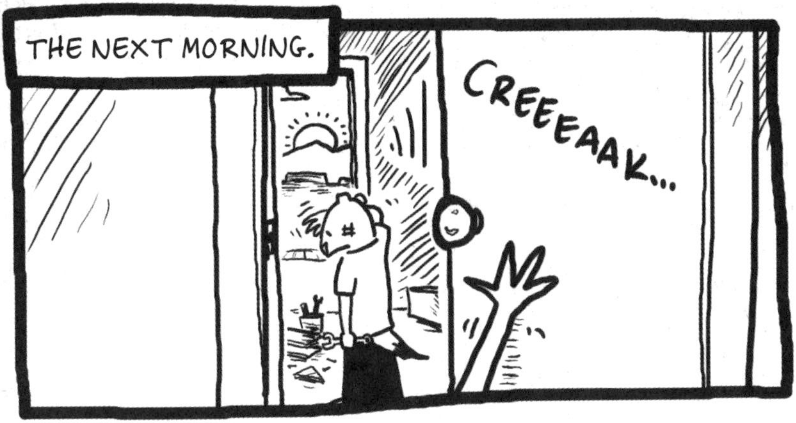
THE NEXT MORNING.
CREEEAAAK...

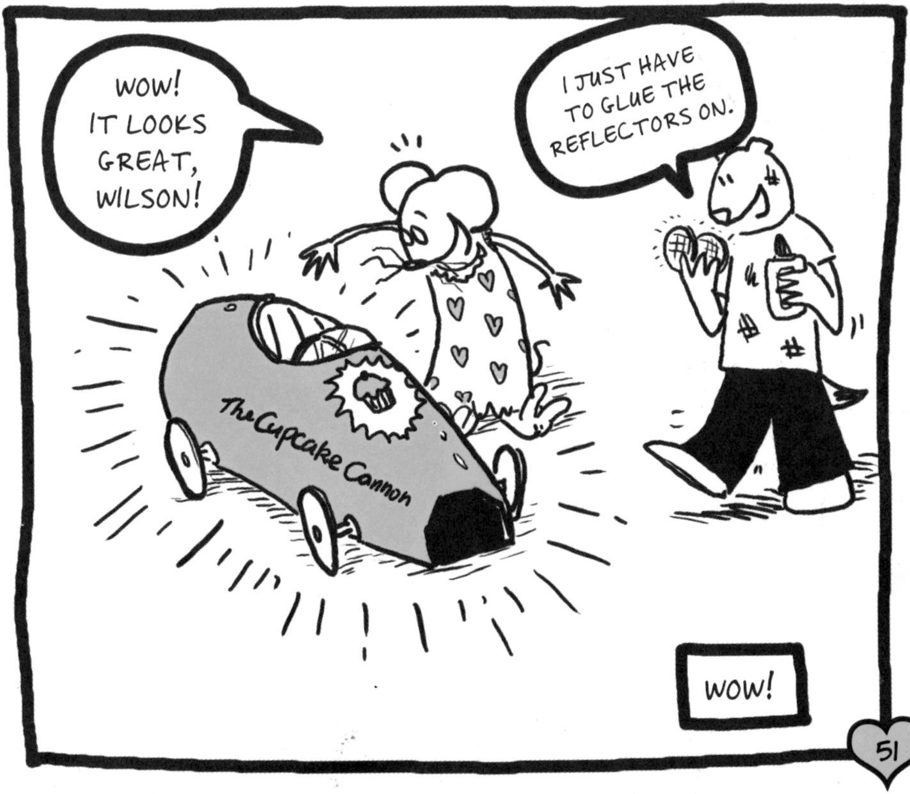
WOW! IT LOOKS GREAT, WILSON!
I JUST HAVE TO GLUE THE REFLECTORS ON.
The Cupcake Cannon
WOW!

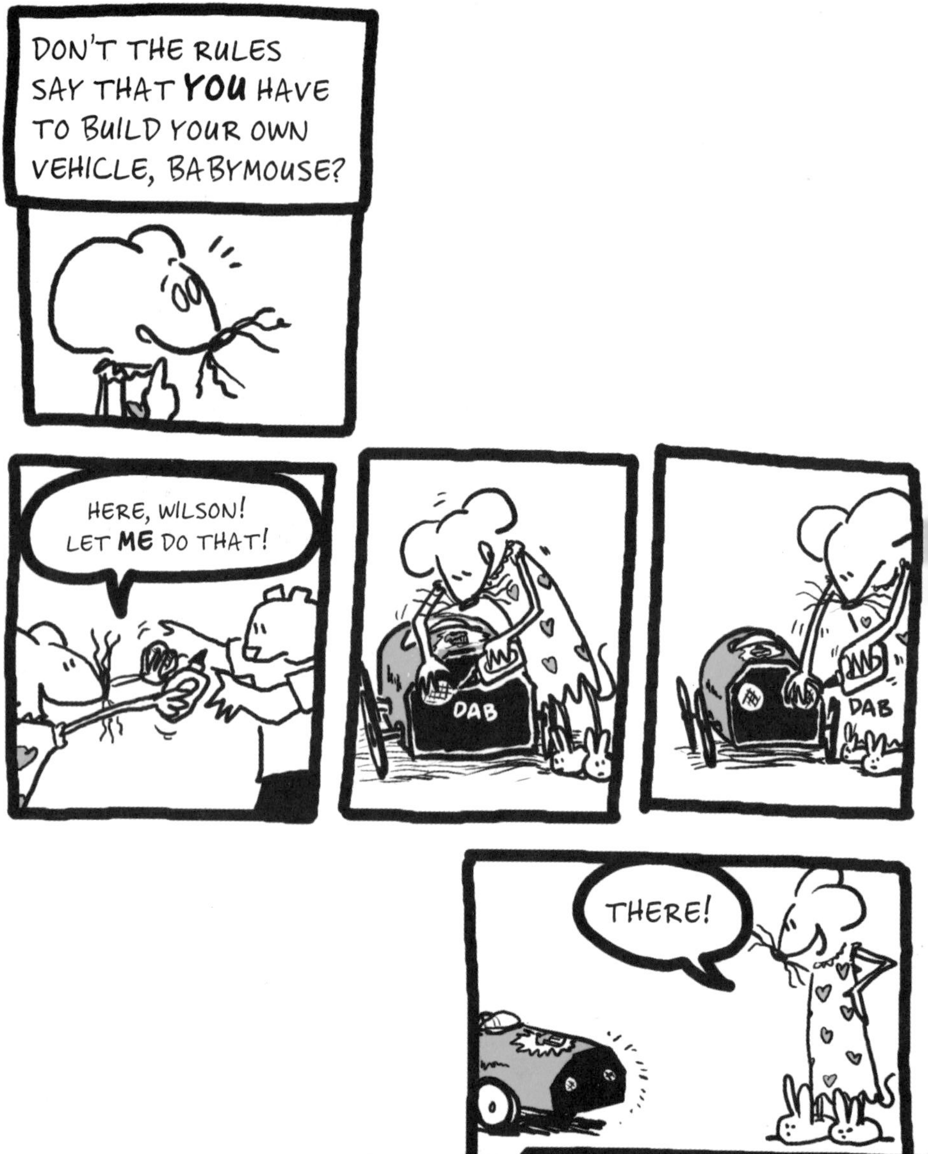
DON'T THE RULES SAY THAT YOU HAVE TO BUILD YOUR OWN VEHICLE, BABYMOUSE?
HERE, WILSON! LET ME DO THAT!
DAB
DAB
THERE!
BOY, I'M TIRED JUST WATCHING YOU, BABYMOUSE.

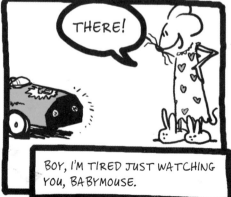

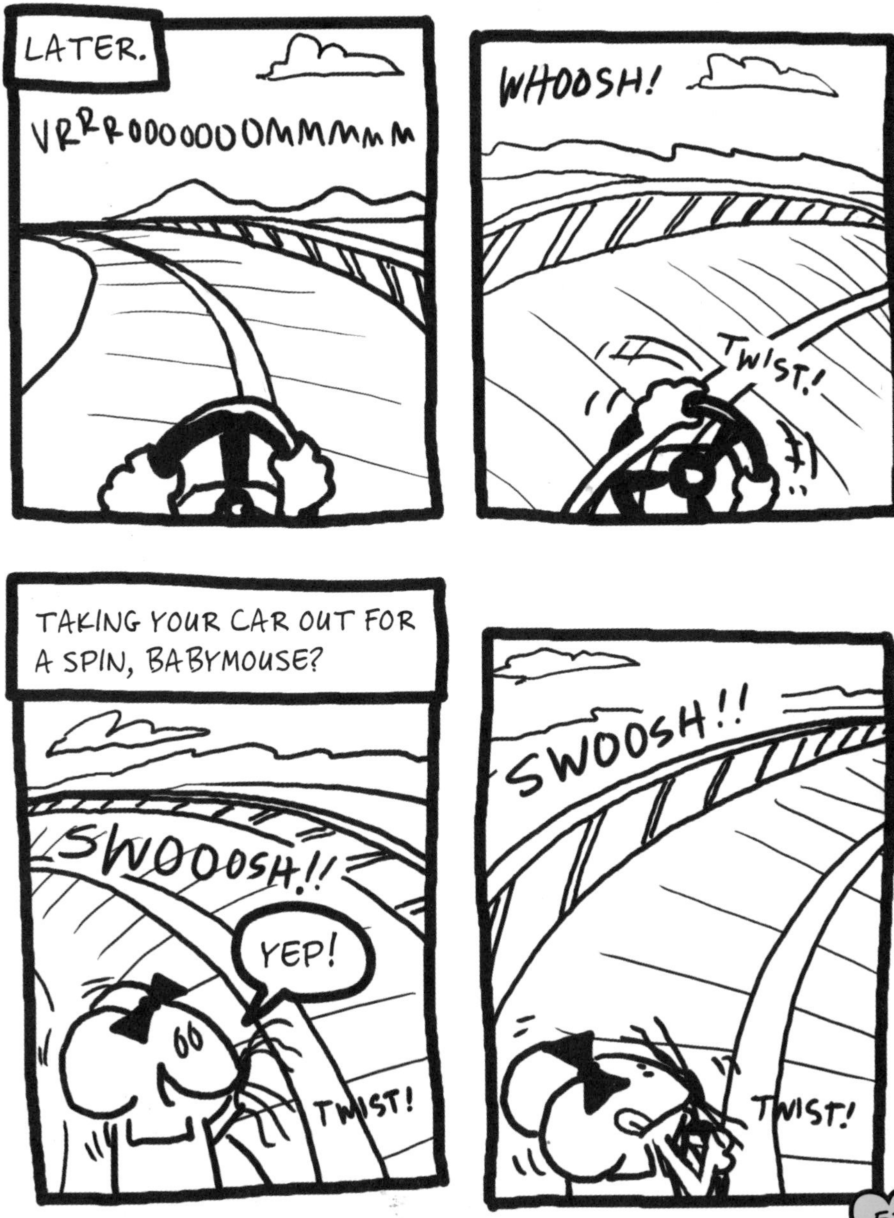
LATER.
VRRROOOOOOOOMMMMMM
WHOOSH!
TWIST!
TAKING YOUR CAR OUT FOR A SPIN, BABYMOUSE?
SWOOOSH!!
YEP!
TWIST!
SWOOSH!!
TWIST!

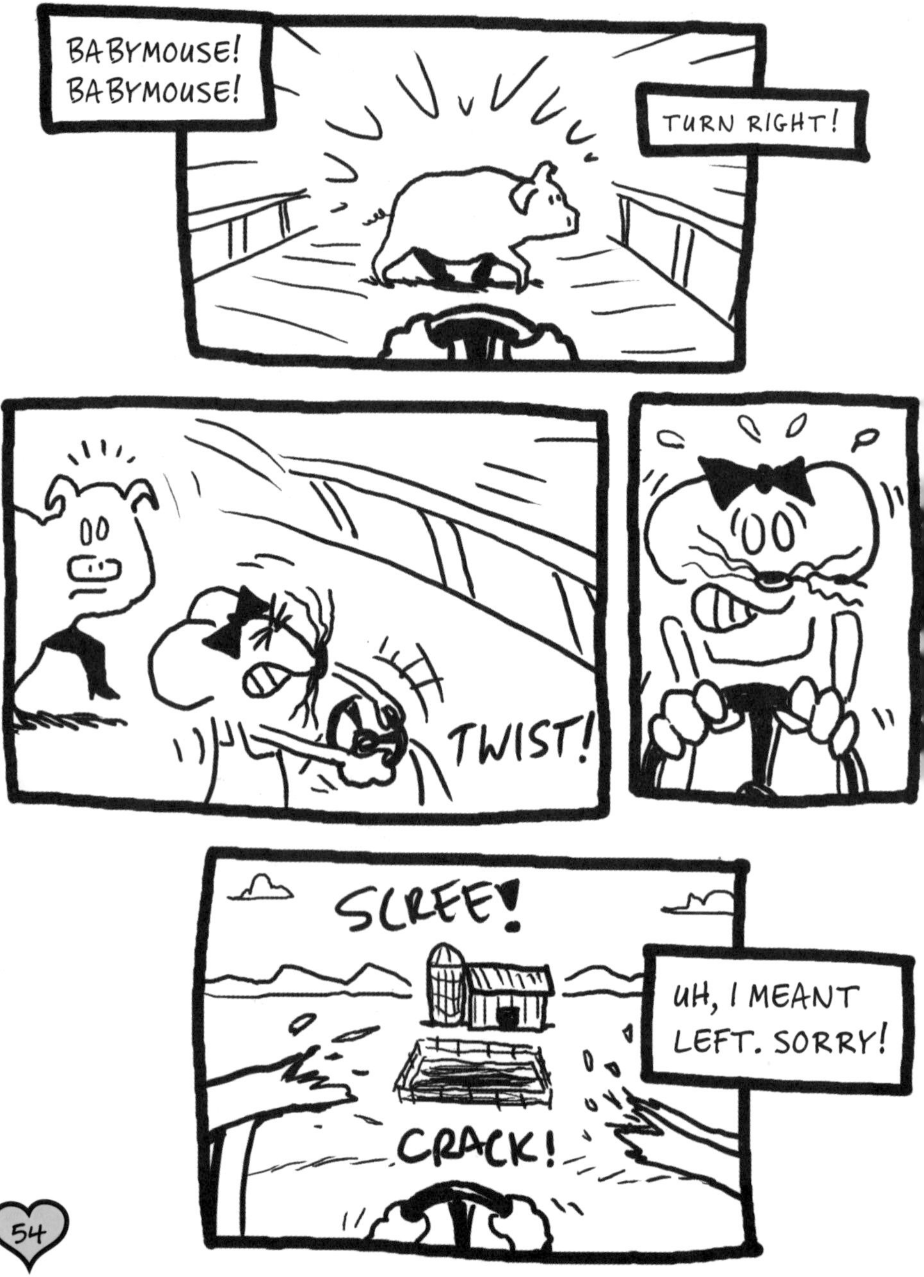
BABYMOUSE! BABYMOUSE!
TURN RIGHT!
TWIST!
SCREE!
UH, I MEANT LEFT. SORRY!
CRACK!

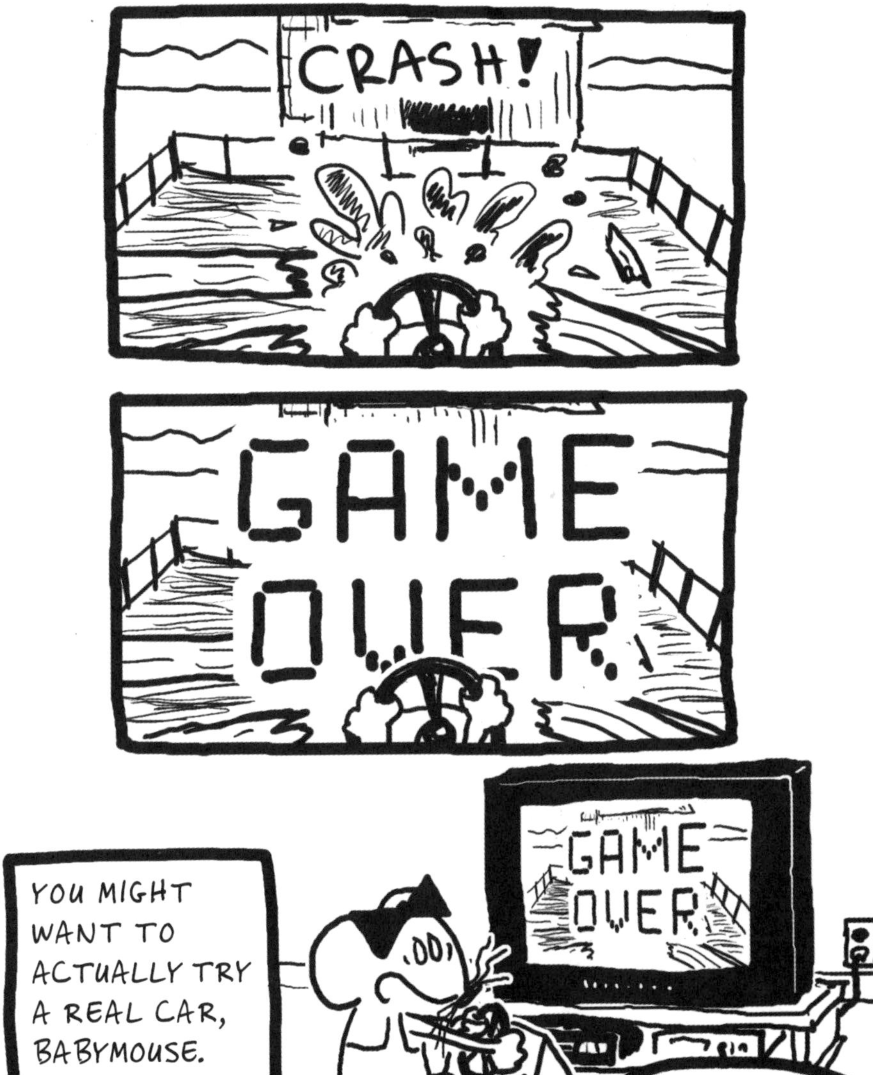
CRASH!
GAME OVER
GAME OVER
YOU MIGHT WANT TO ACTUALLY TRY A REAL CAR, BABYMOUSE.
BUT THE BOX SAID IT WAS GOOD FOR DEVELOPING HAND-EYE COORDINATION!

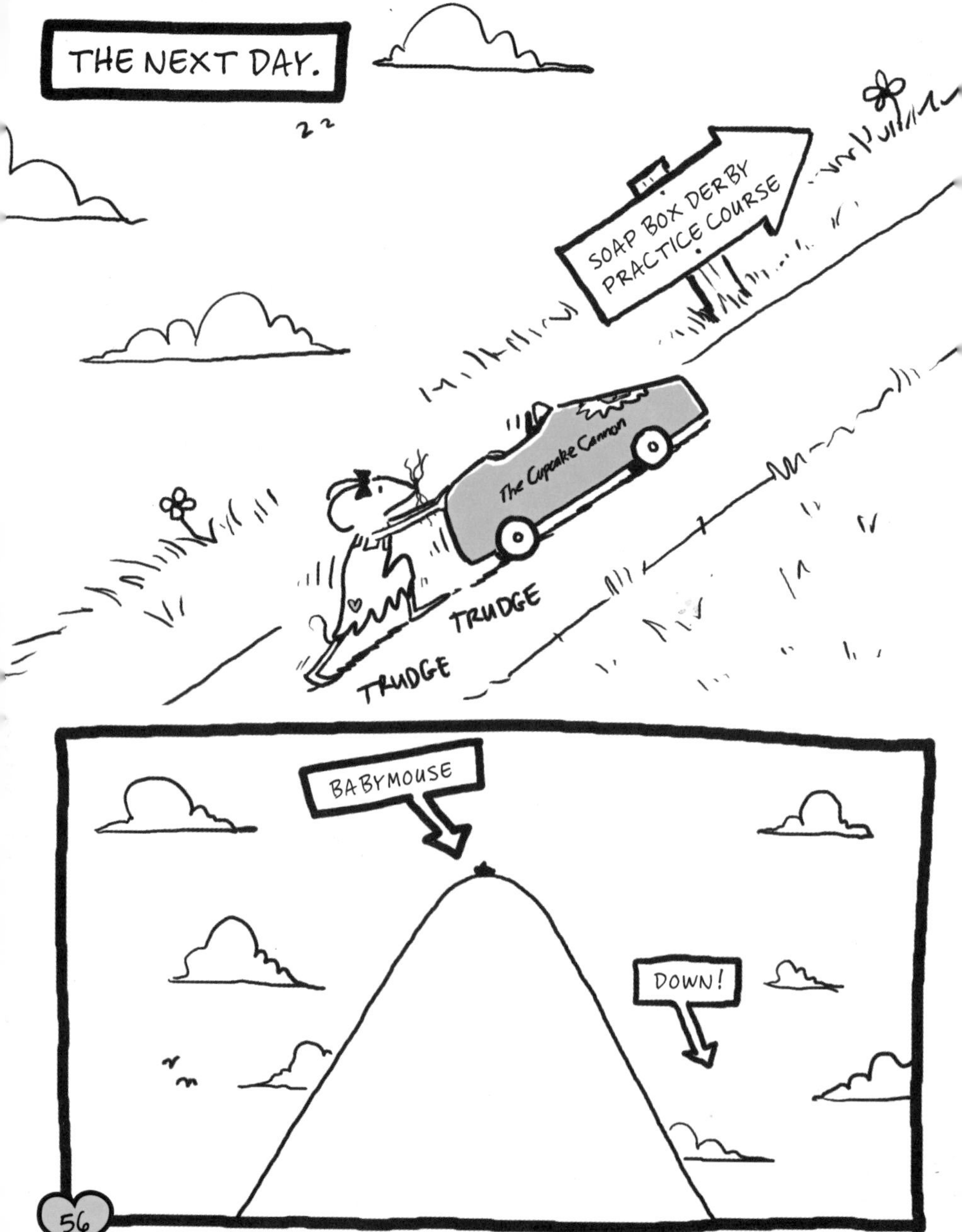
THE NEXT DAY.
SOAP BOX DERBY PRACTICE COURSE
The Cupcake Cannon
TRUDGE
TRUDGE
BABYMOUSE
DOWN!

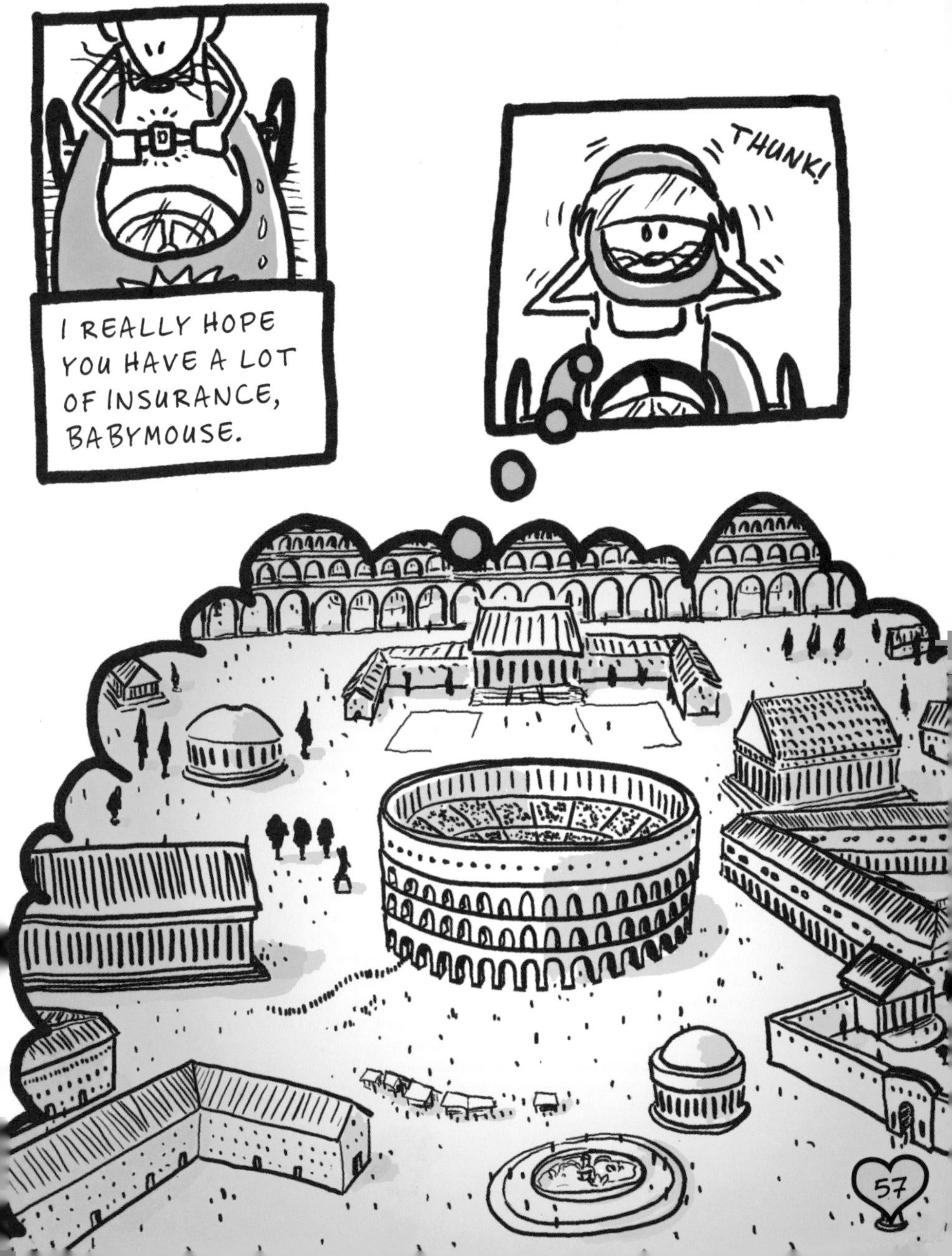
I REALLY HOPE YOU HAVE A LOT OF INSURANCE, BABYMOUSE.
THUNK!

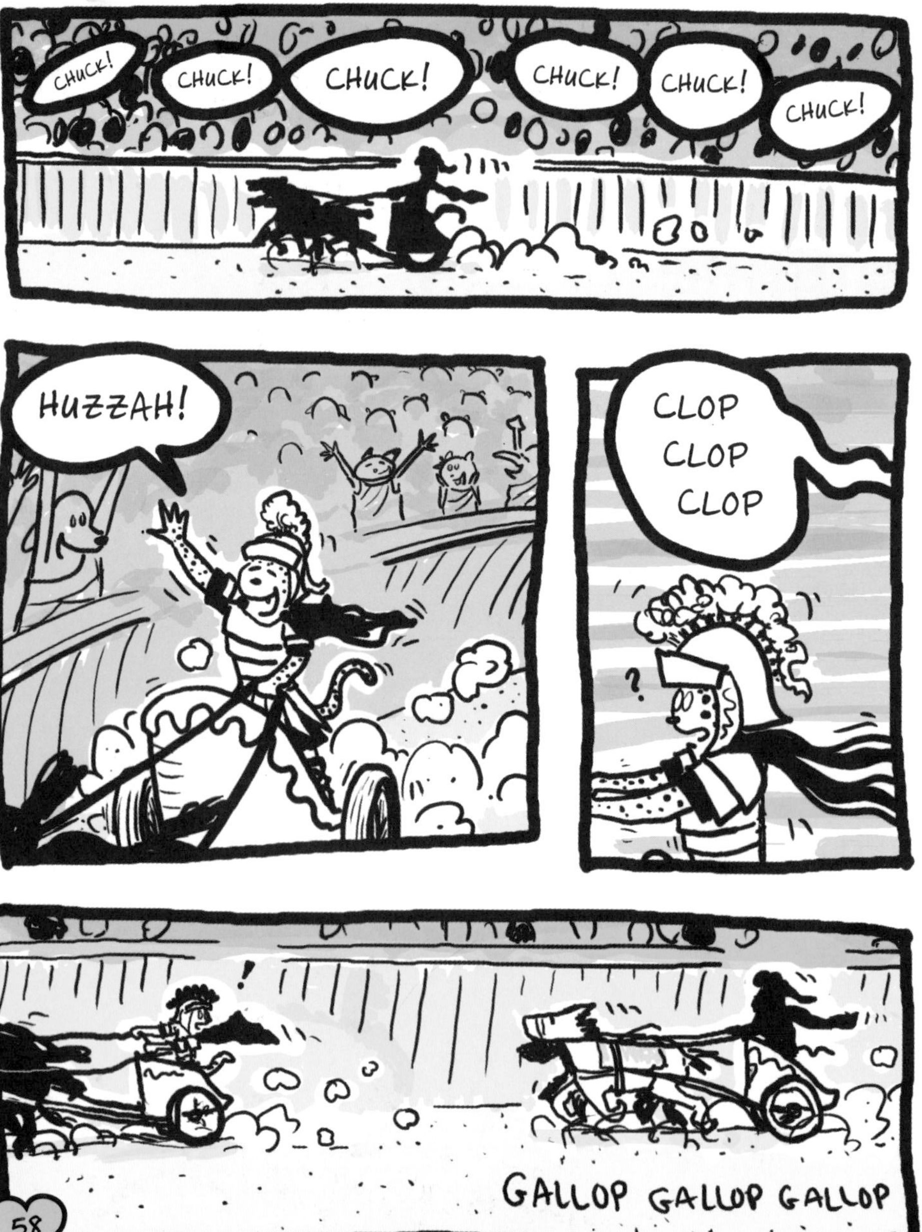
CHUCK!
CHUCK!
CHUCK!
CHUCK!
CHUCK!
CHUCK!
HUZZAH!
CLOP CLOP CLOP
?
!
GALLOP GALLOP GALLOP

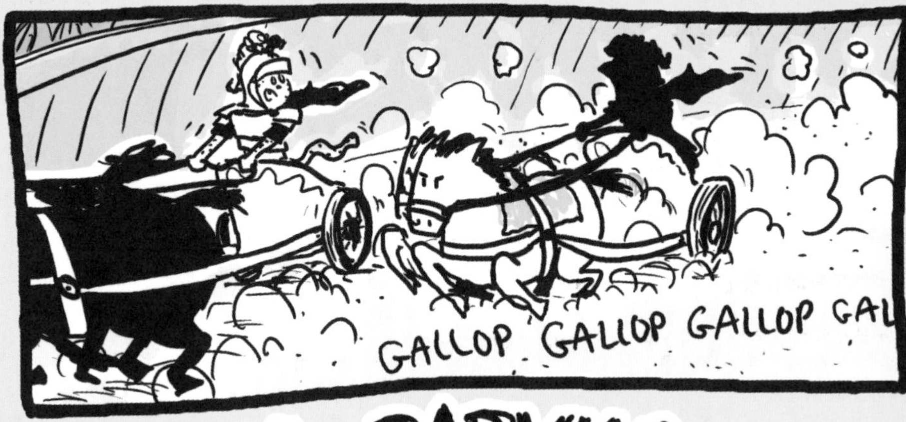
GALLOP GALLOP GALLOP GAL

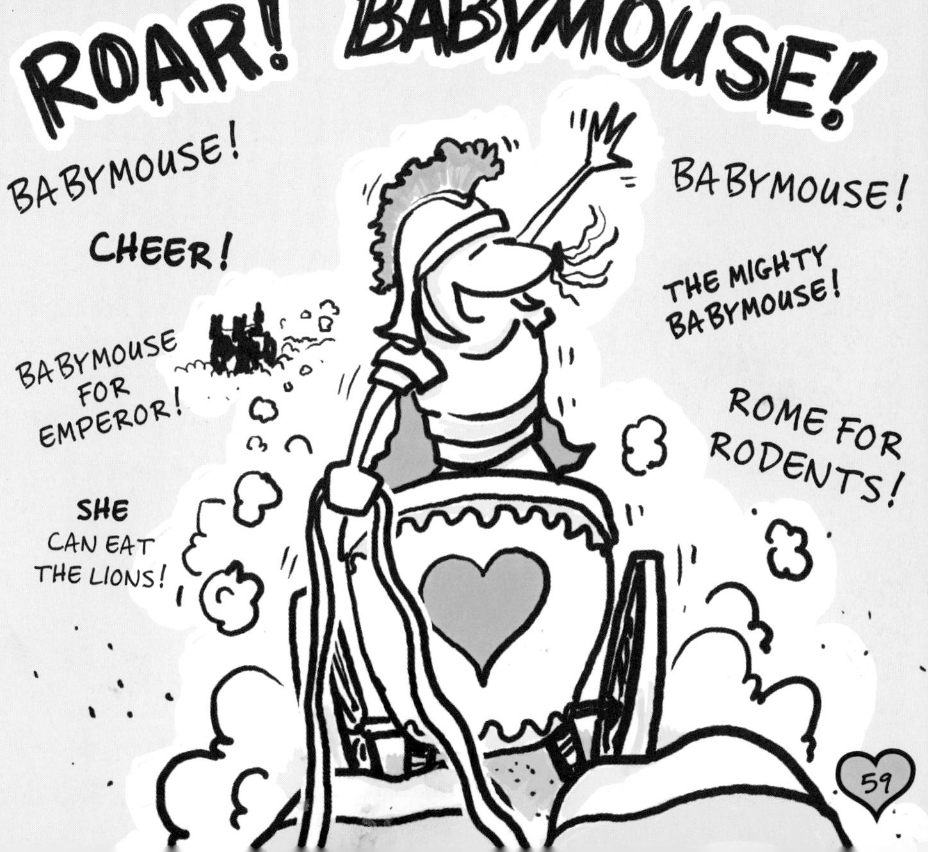
ROAR! BABYMOUSE!
BABYMOUSE!
BABYMOUSE!
CHEER!
THE MIGHTY BABYMOUSE!
BABYMOUSE FOR EMPEROR!
ROME FOR RODENTS!
SHE CAN EAT THE LIONS!

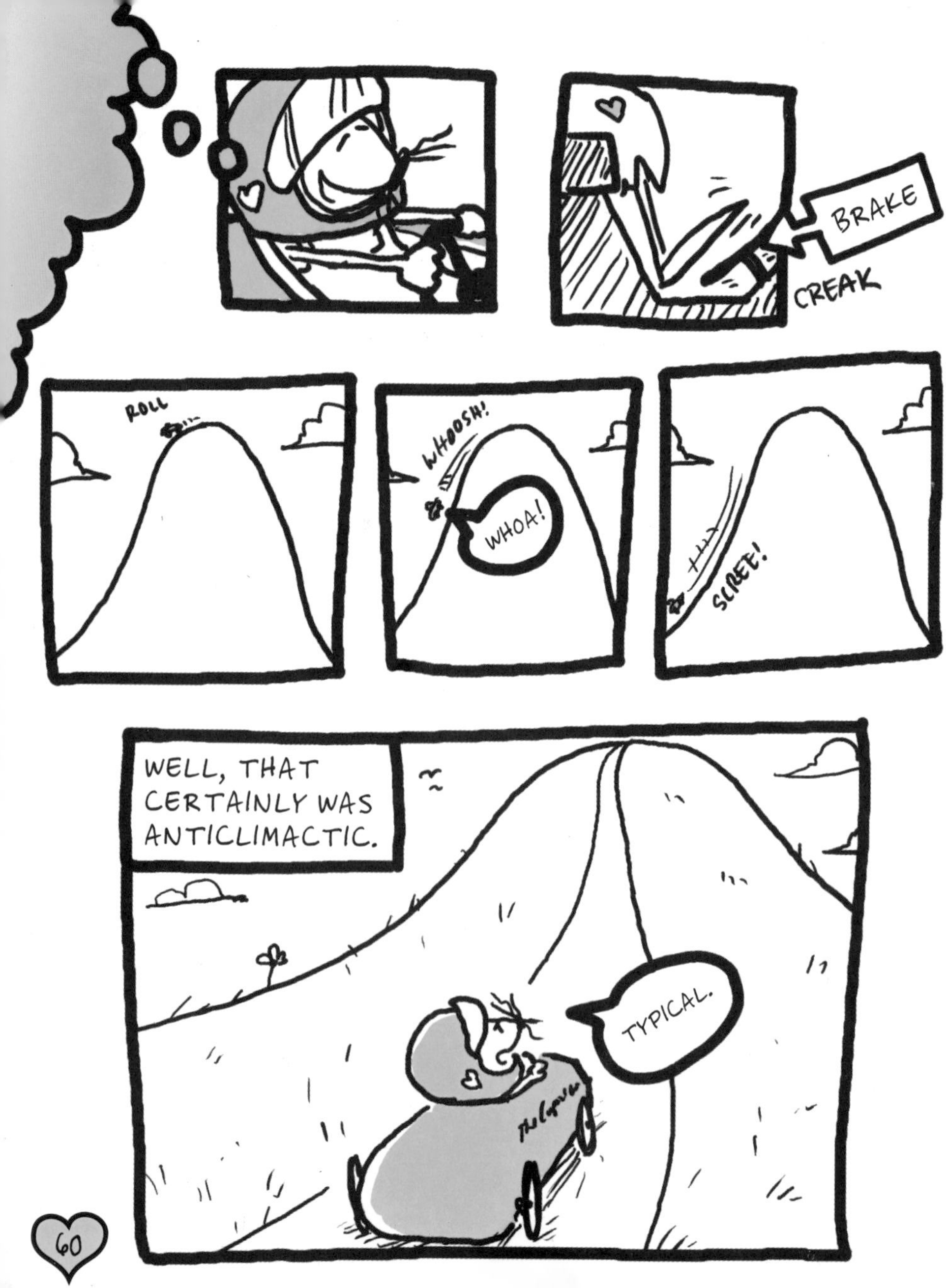
BRAKE
CREAK
ROLL
WHOOSH!
WHOA!
SCREE!
WELL, THAT CERTAINLY WAS ANTICLIMACTIC.
TYPICAL.

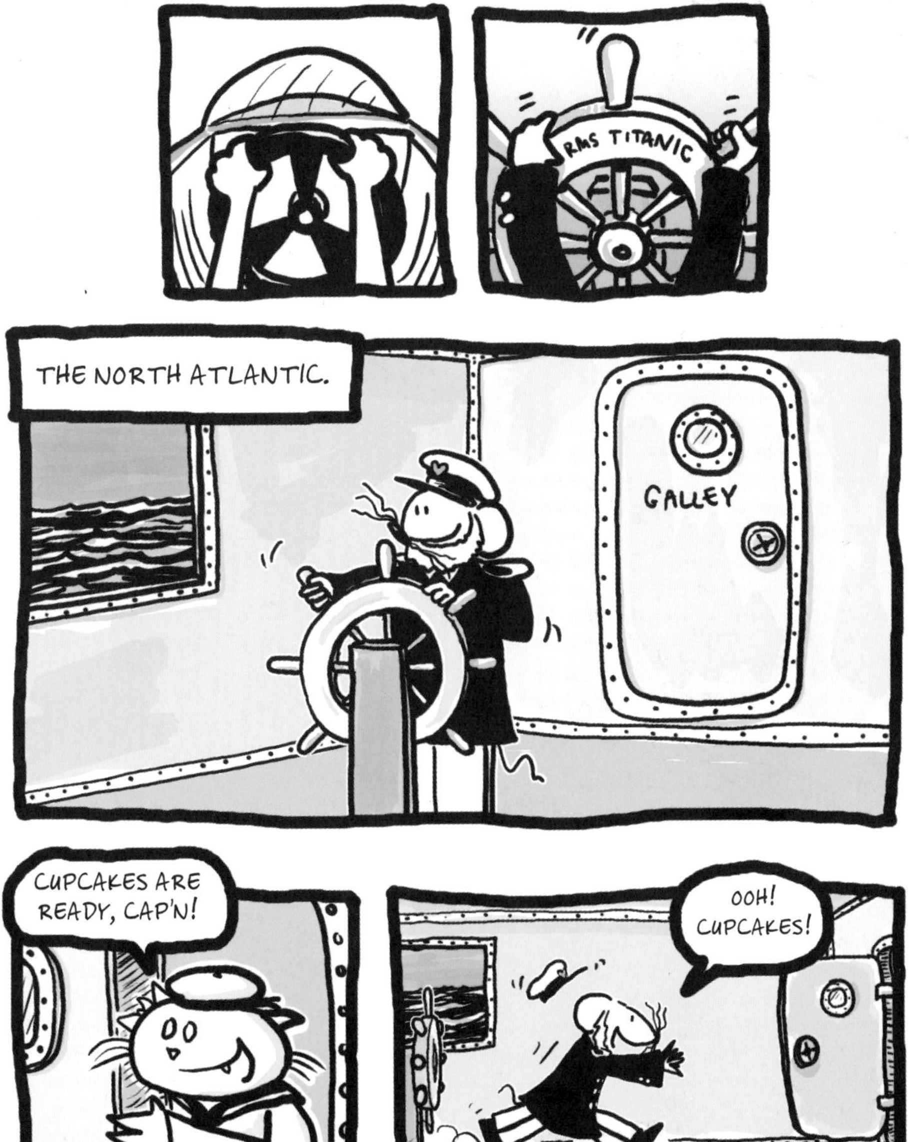
RMS TITANIC
THE NORTH ATLANTIC.
GALLEY
CUPCAKES ARE READY, CAP'N!
OOH! CUPCAKES!

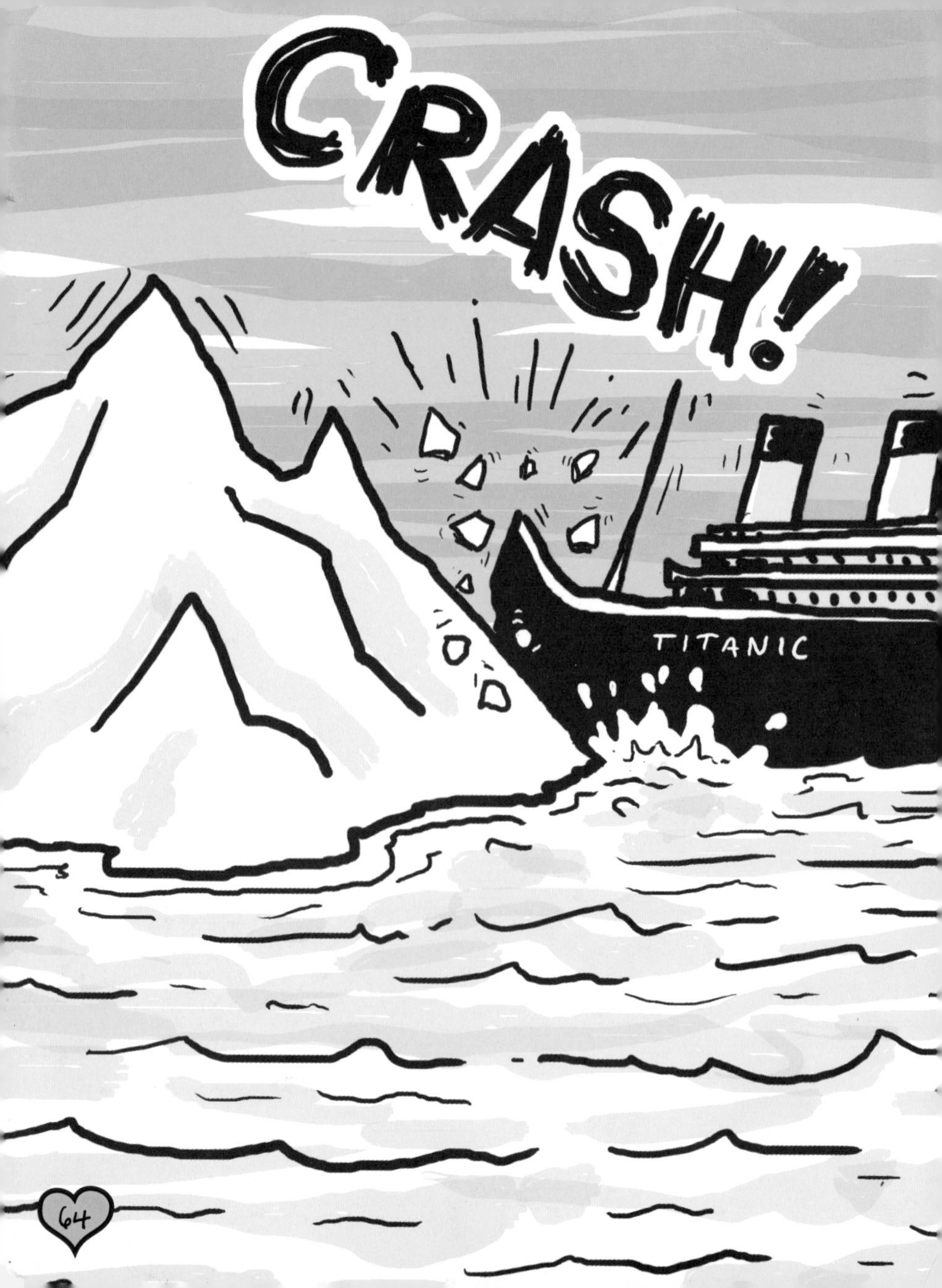
CRASH!
TITANIC

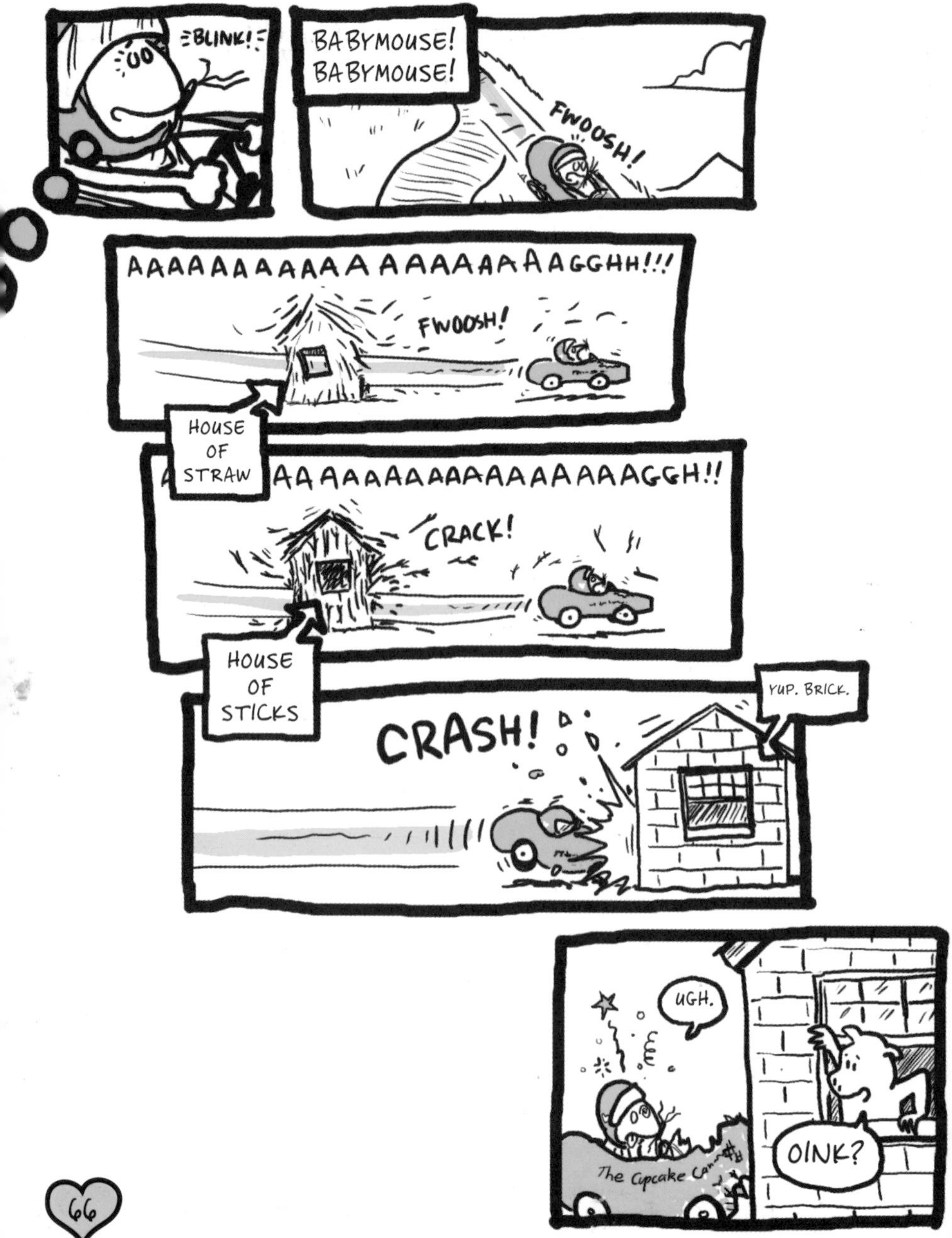
BLINK!
BABYMOUSE! BABYMOUSE!
FWOOSH!
AAAAAAAAAAAAAAAAAAAGGHH!!!
FWOOSH!
HOUSE OF STRAW
AAAAAAAAAAAAAAAAAAAAAGGH!!
CRACK!
HOUSE OF STICKS
CRASH!
YUP. BRICK.
UGH.
The Cupcake Ca
OINK?

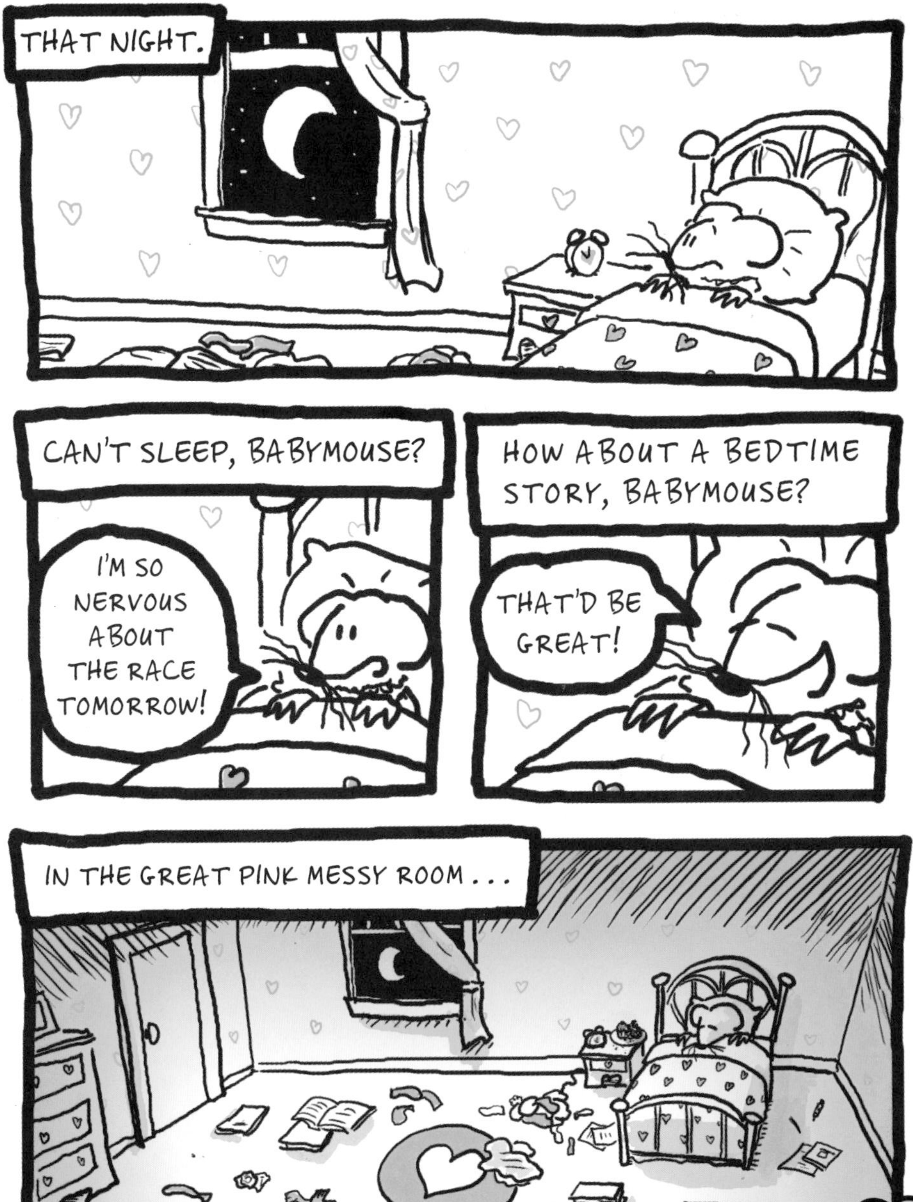
THAT NIGHT.
CAN'T SLEEP, BABYMOUSE?
I'M SO NERVOUS ABOUT THE RACE TOMORROW!
HOW ABOUT A BEDTIME STORY, BABYMOUSE?
THAT'D BE GREAT!
IN THE GREAT PINK MESSY ROOM . . .

CHAPTER VII
A NEW CUPCAKE

It is a dark time for the REBELLION. The brave pilot, BABYMOUSE, has badgered her best friend into building her a SOAP BOX DERBY CAR.

SOAP BOX DERBY CAR.

Little does she know that the
villainous CHUCK E. CHEETAH is
going to totally mop the floor
with her, since he has actually
practiced every day for years
and she can't avoid crashing
into pigpens.

into pigpens.

Now the hour has come at last
that will spell certain doom
for the blah blah blah blah...
are you still reading this?

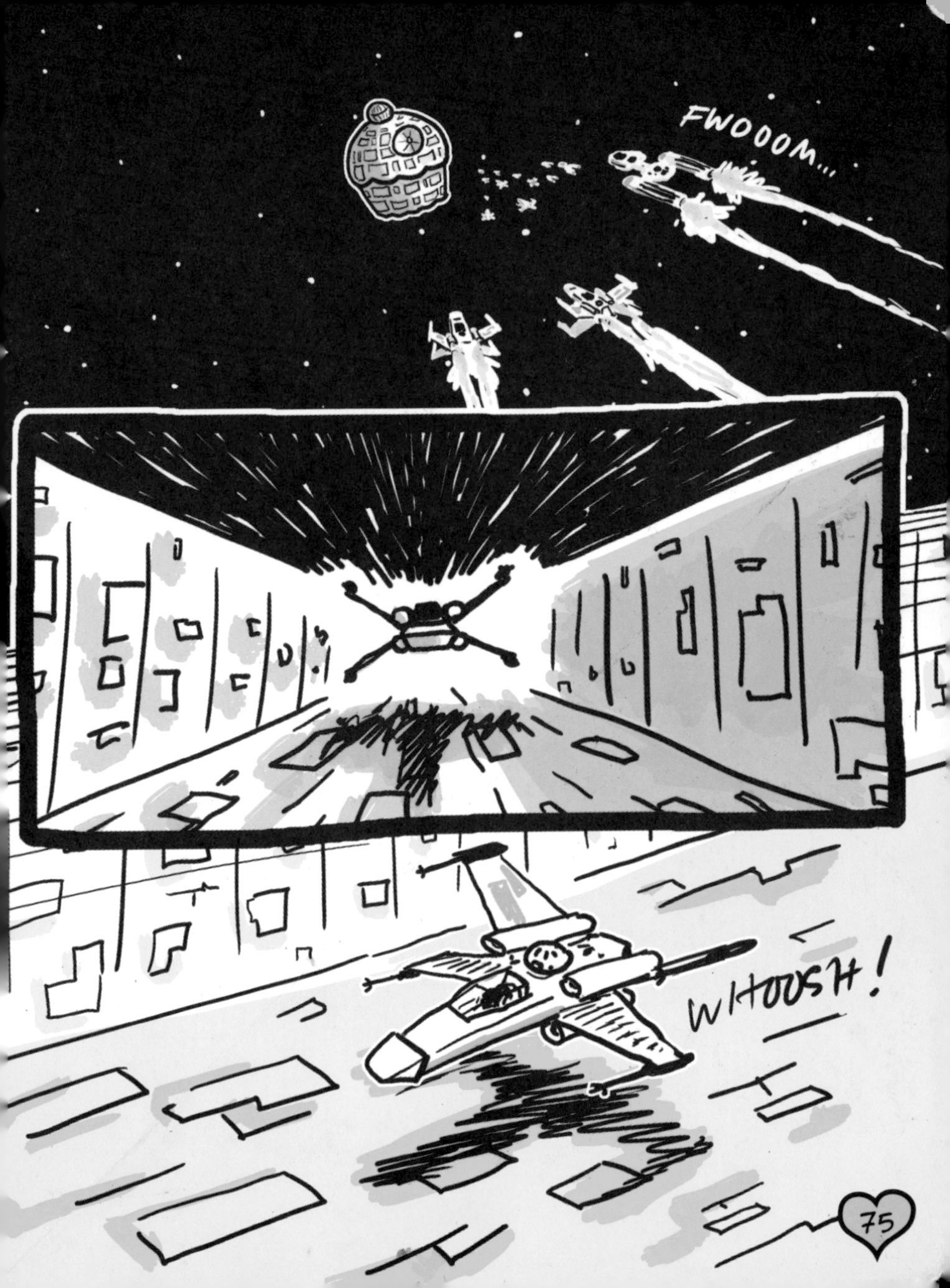
FWOOOM...
WHOOSH!

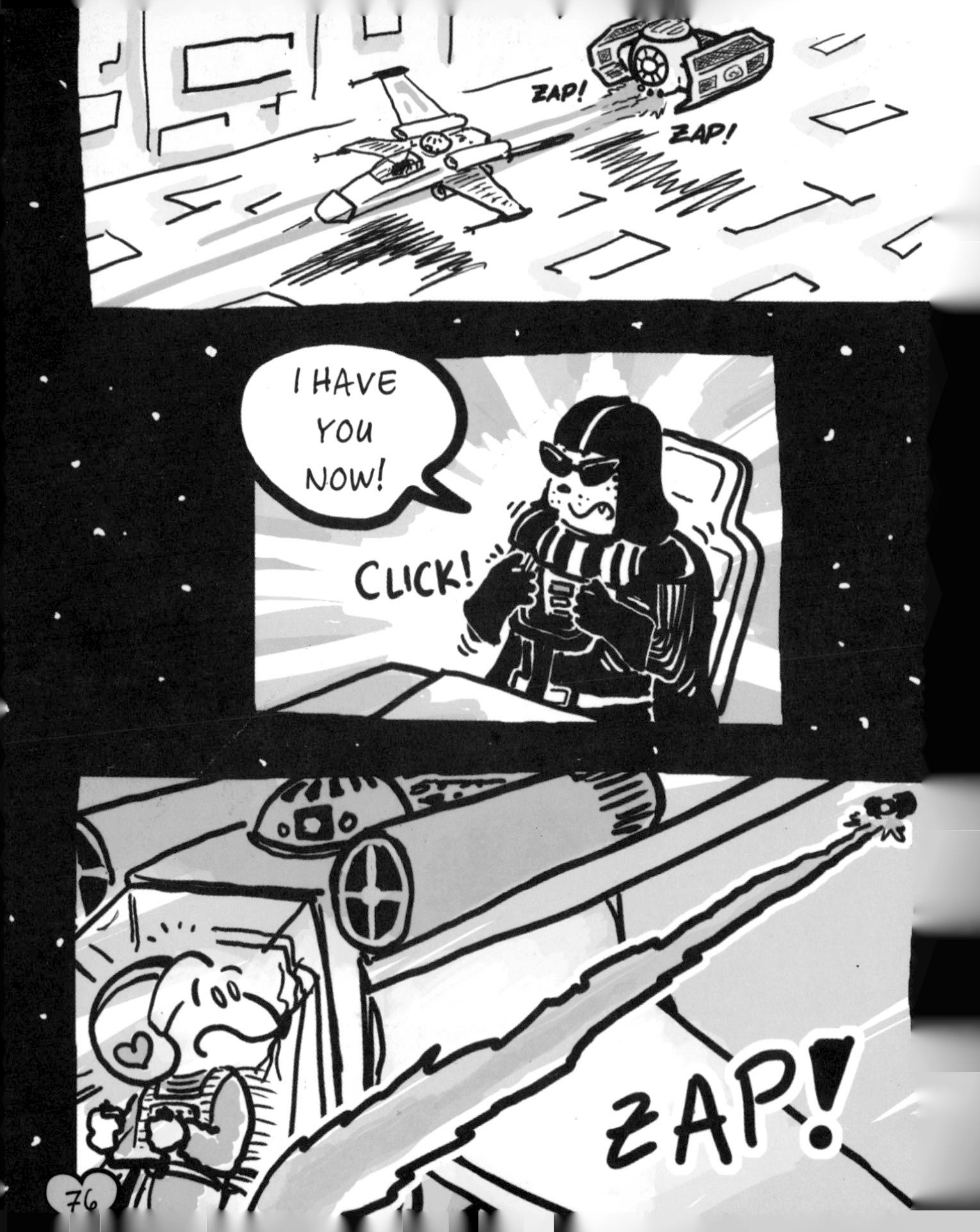
ZAP!
ZAP!
I HAVE YOU NOW!
CLICK!
ZAP!

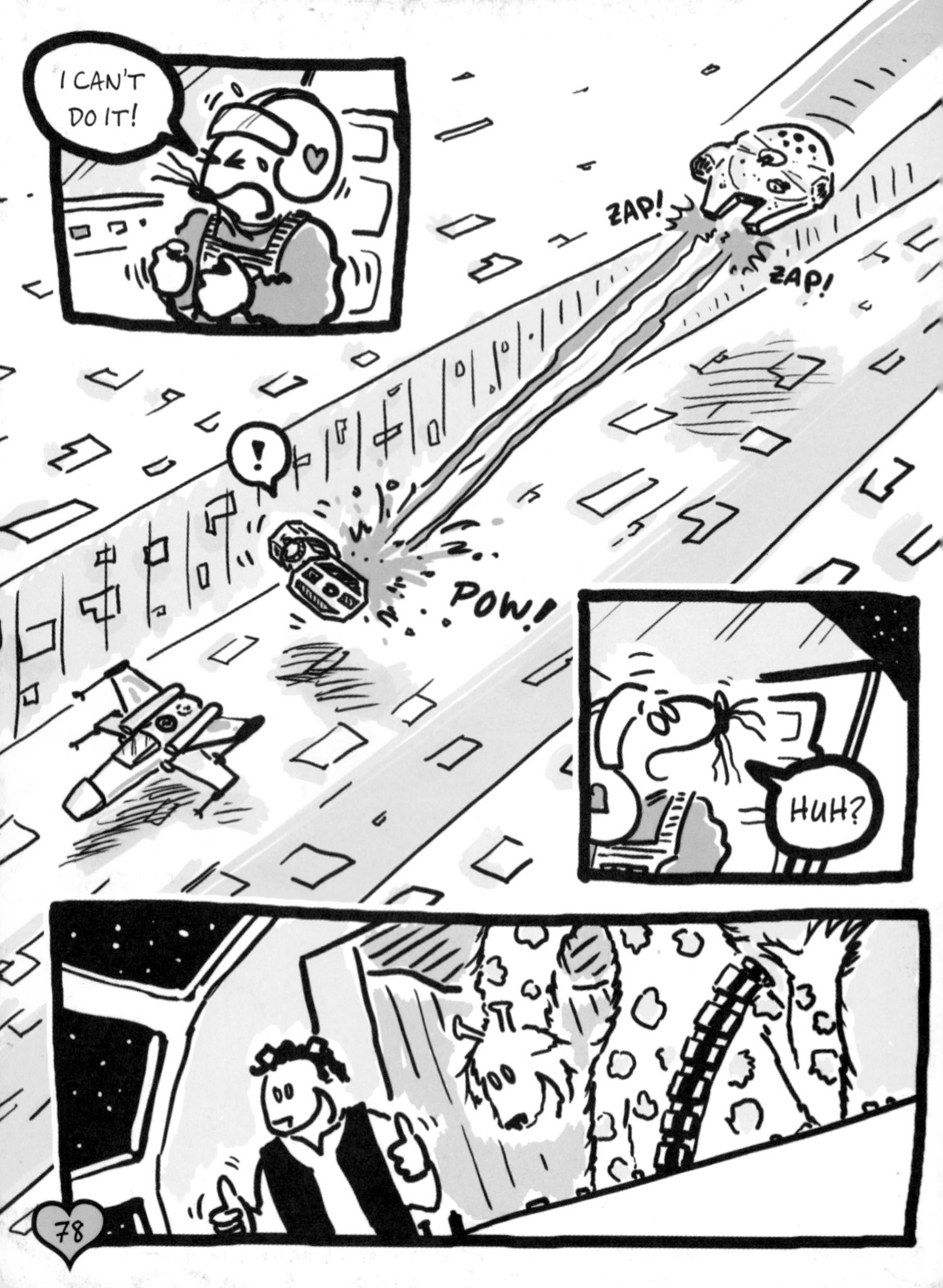

I CAN'T DO IT!
ZAP!
ZAP!
!
POW!
HUH?

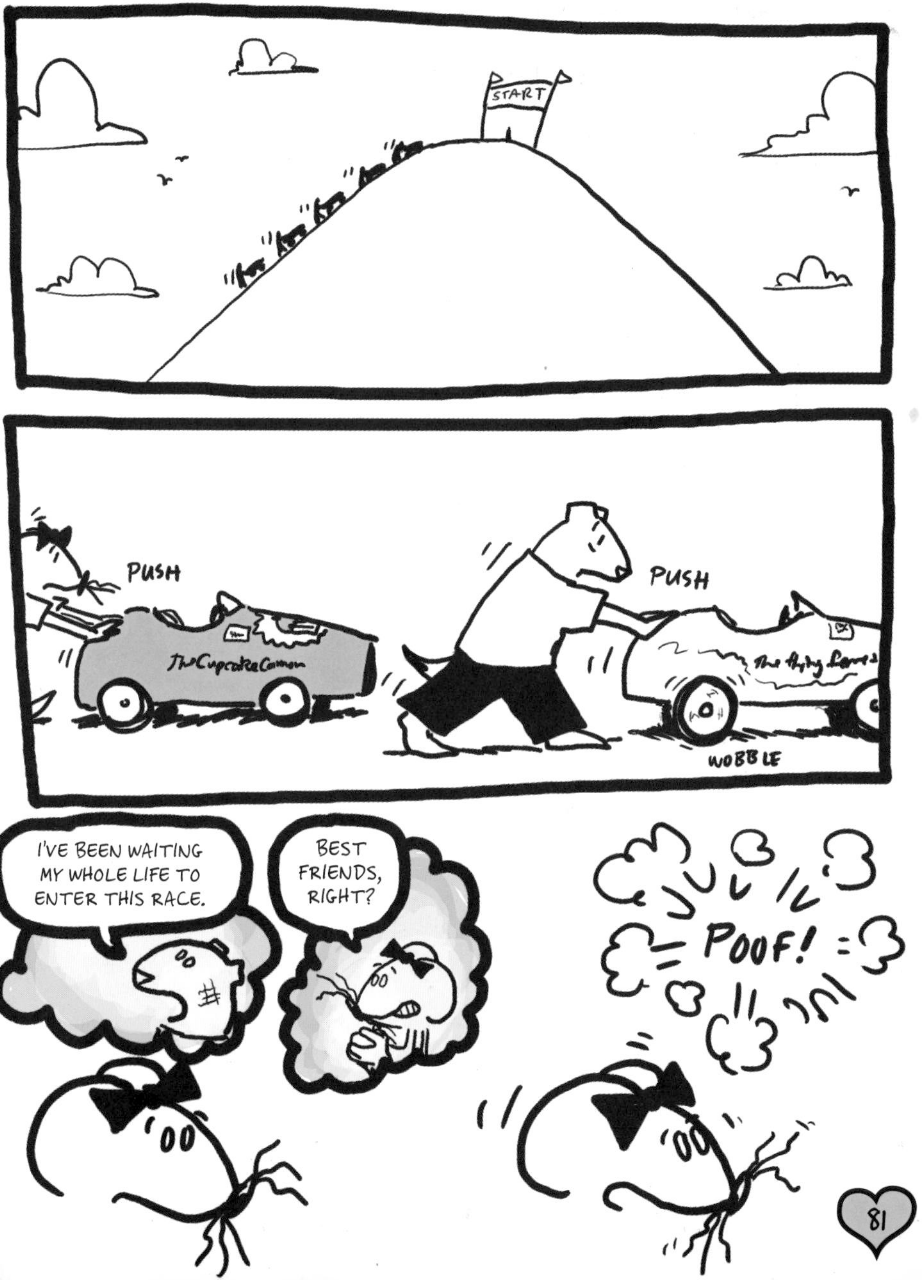
START
PUSH
The Cupcake Cannon
PUSH
WOBBLE
I'VE BEEN WAITING MY WHOLE LIFE TO ENTER THIS RACE.
BEST FRIENDS, RIGHT?
POOF!

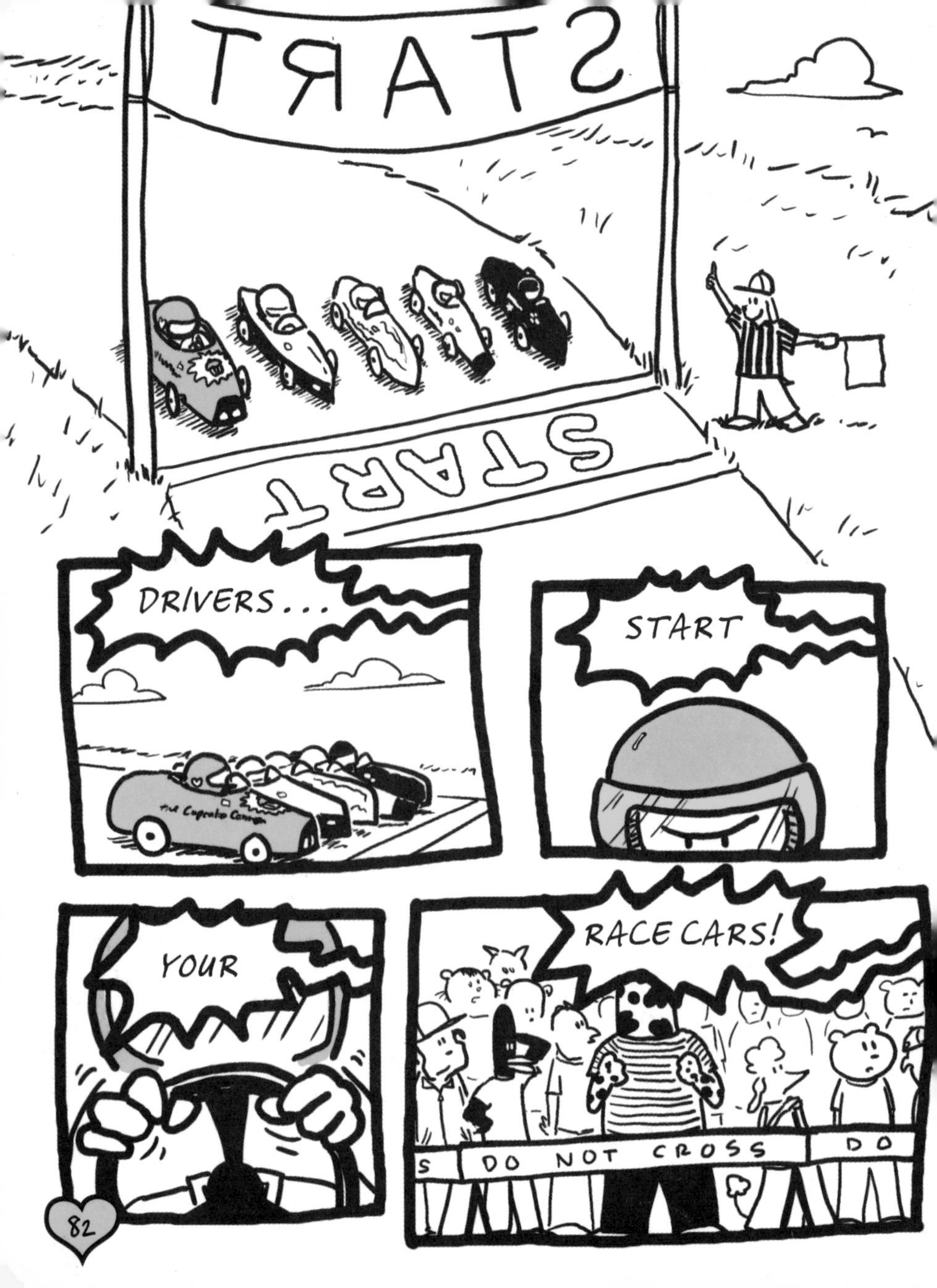
START
START
DRIVERS . . .
the Cupcake Cannon
START
YOUR
RACE CARS!
S
DO NOT CROSS
DO

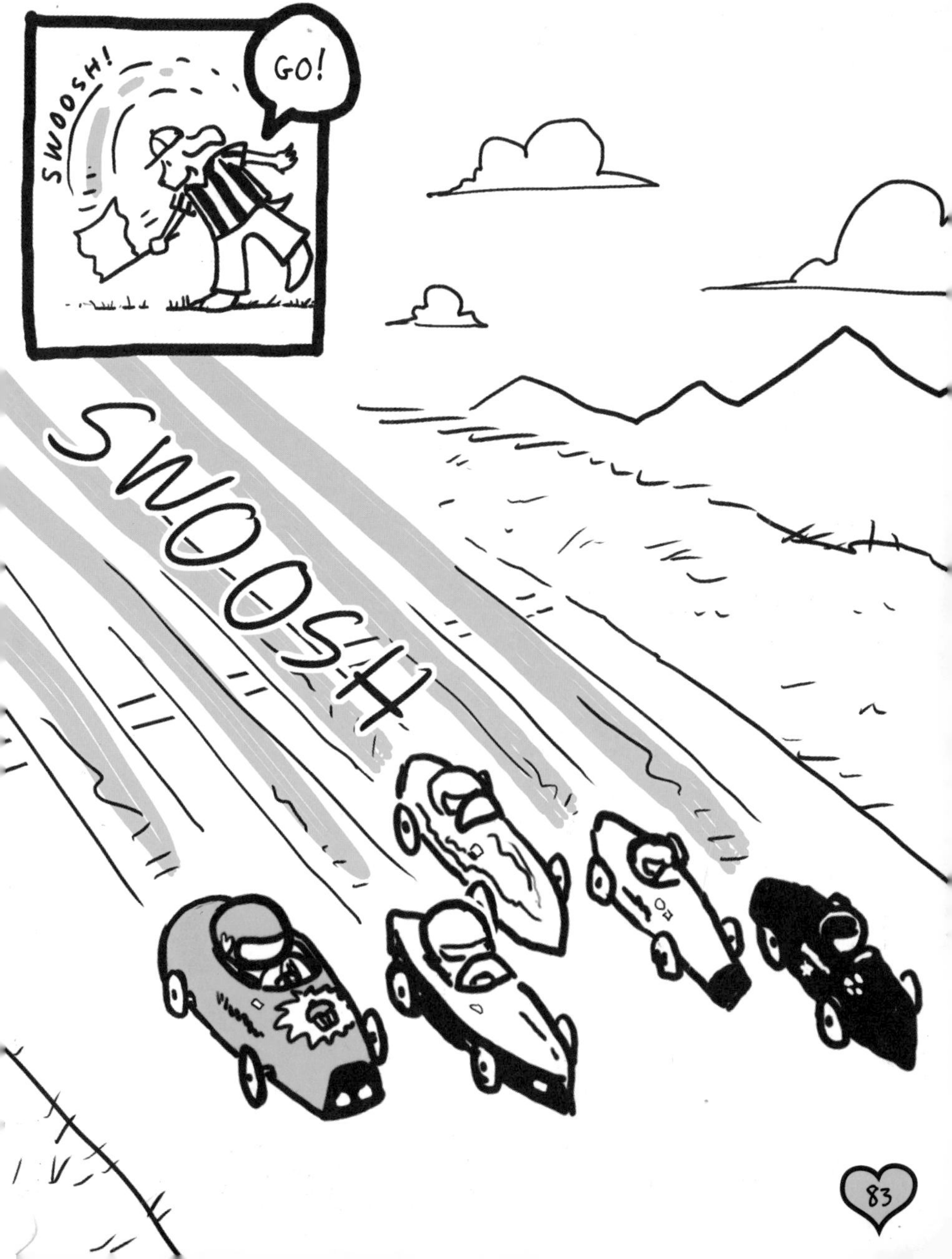
SWOOSH!
GO!
SWOOSH

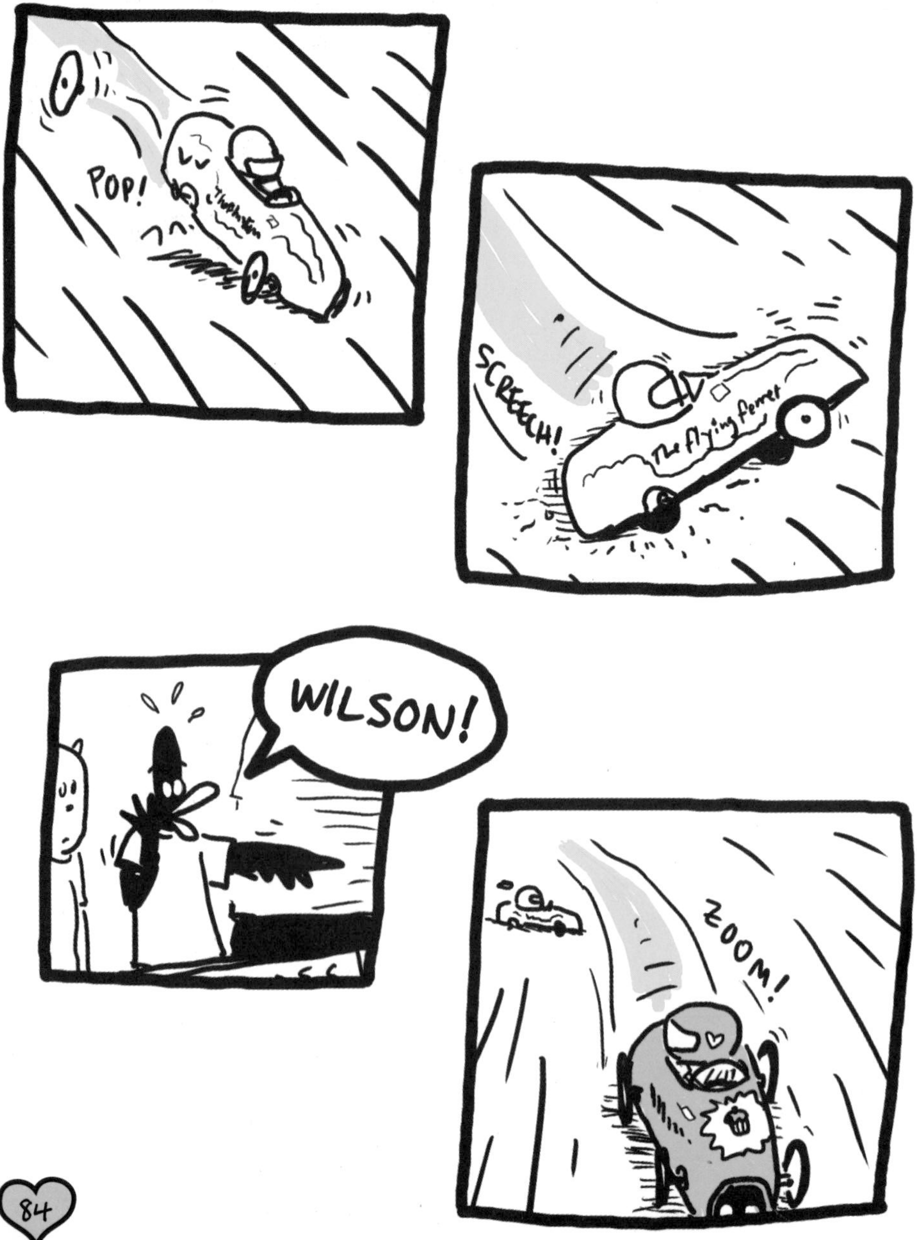
POP!
SCREECH!
The flying ferret
WILSON!
ZOOM!

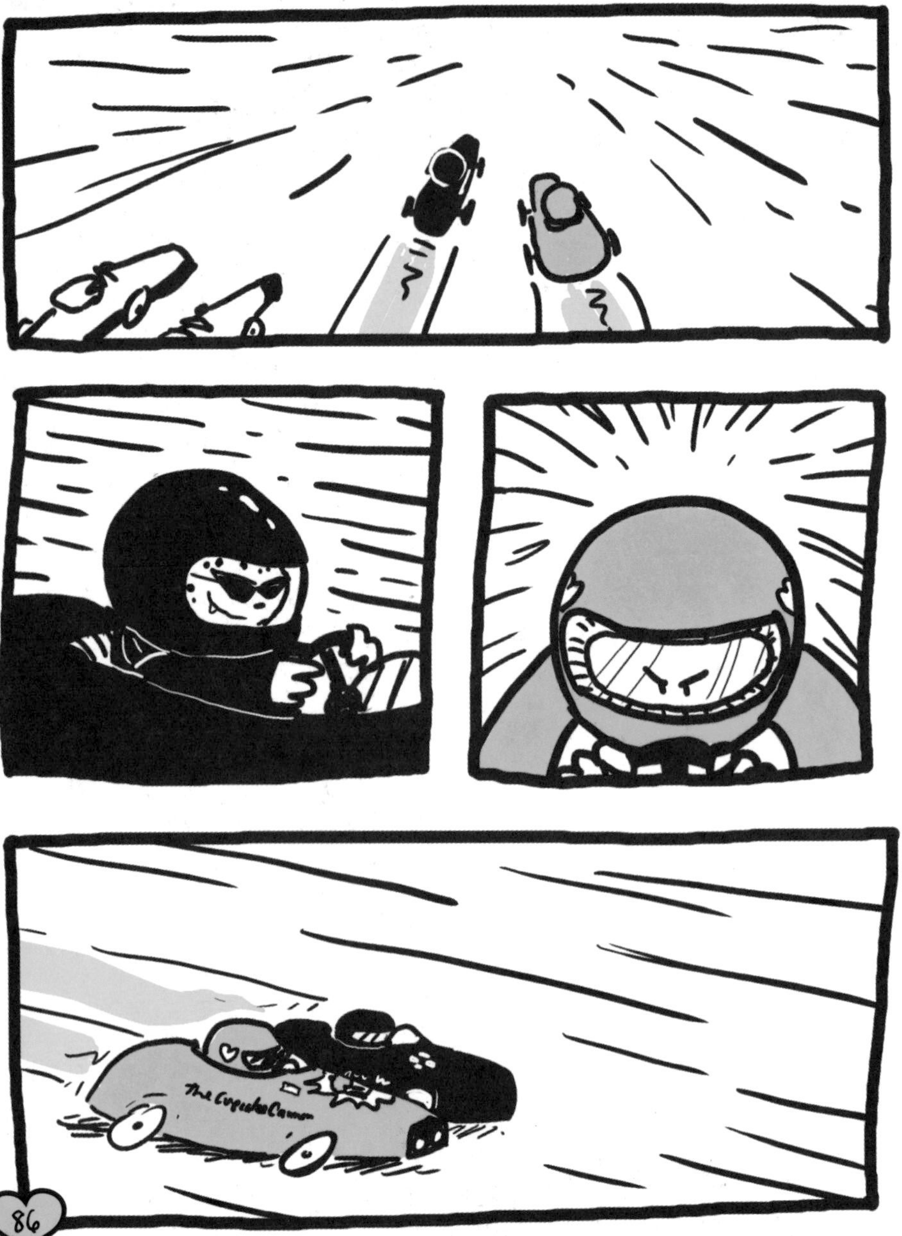
The Cupcake Cannon

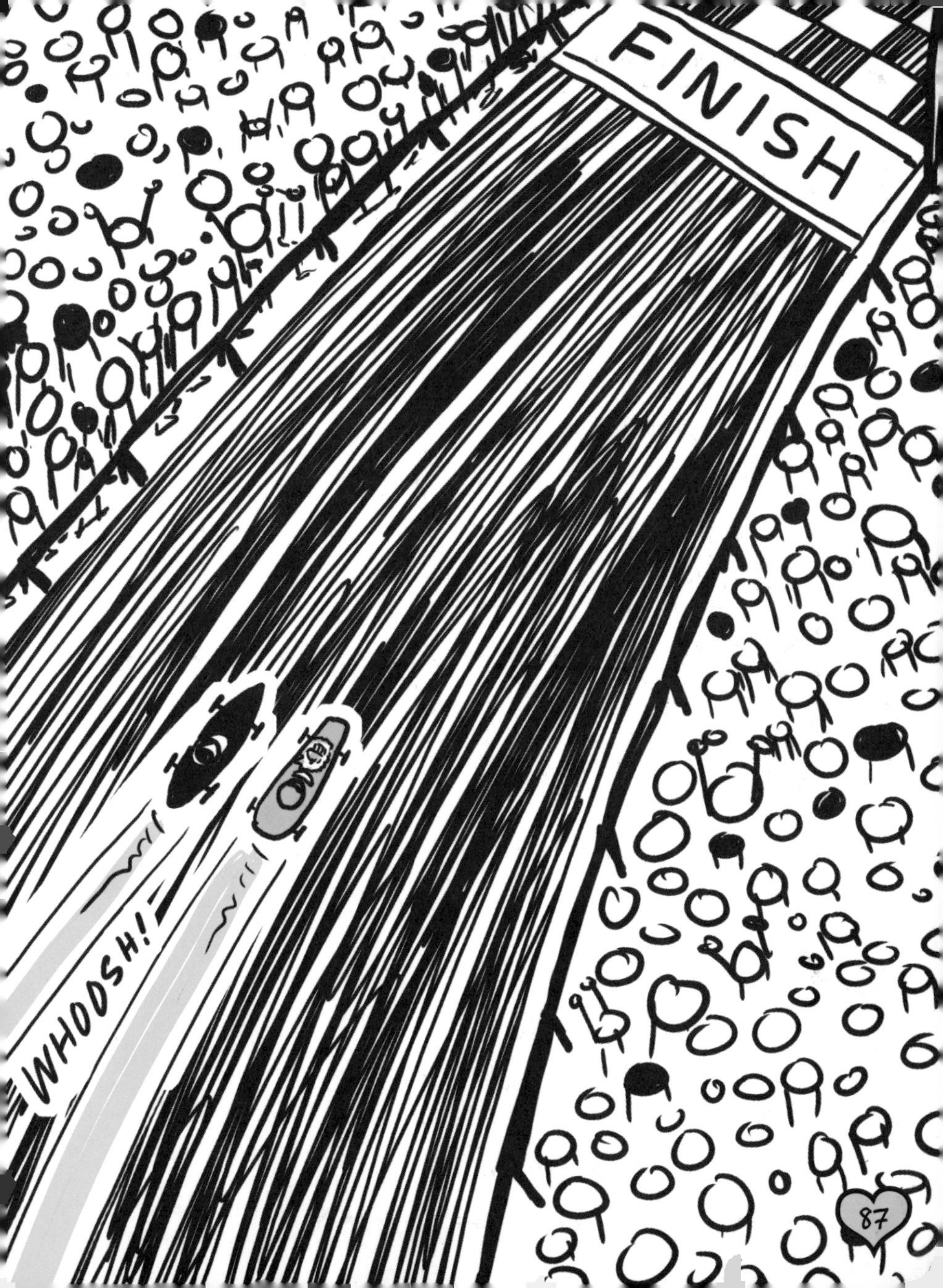
FINISH
WHOOSH!

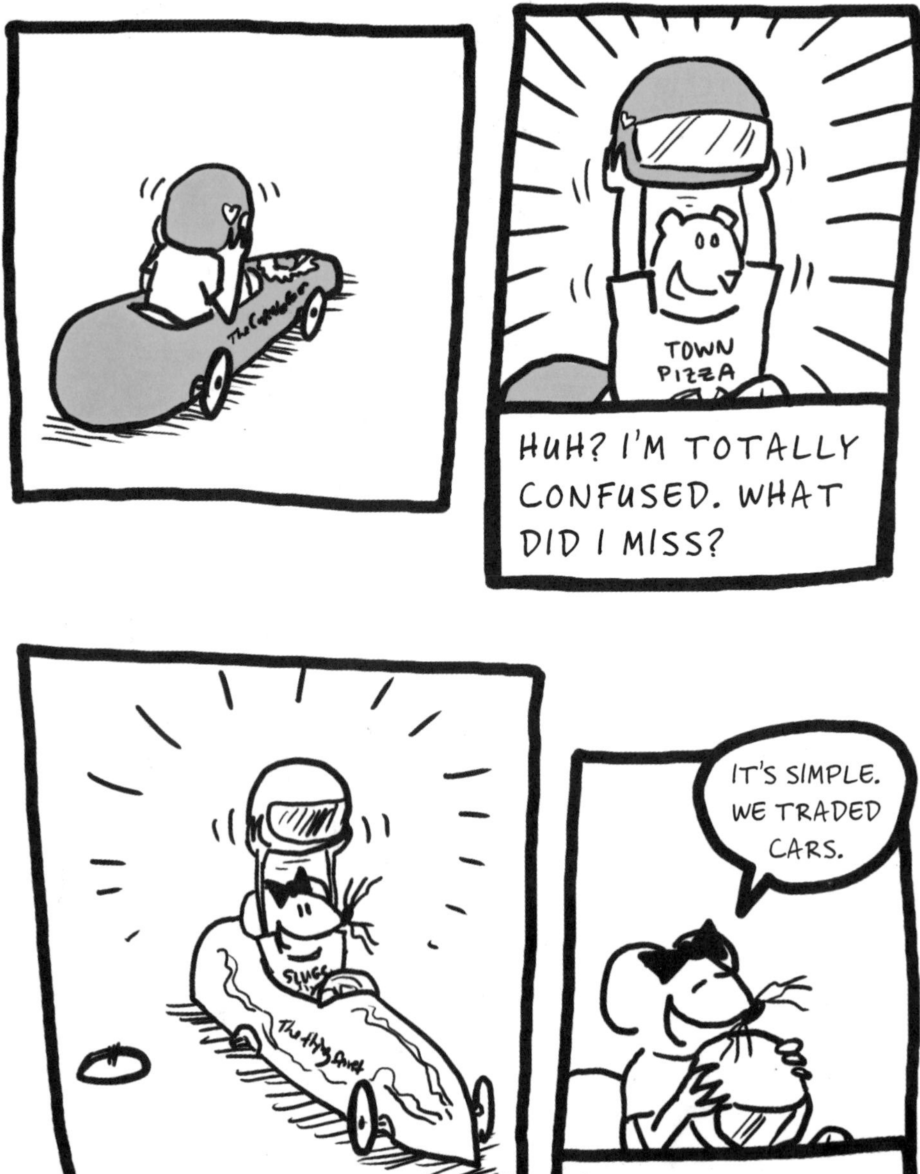
TOWN PIZZA
HUH? I'M TOTALLY CONFUSED. WHAT DID I MISS?
IT'S SIMPLE. WE TRADED CARS.
I'M TEARING UP HERE. SNIFF.

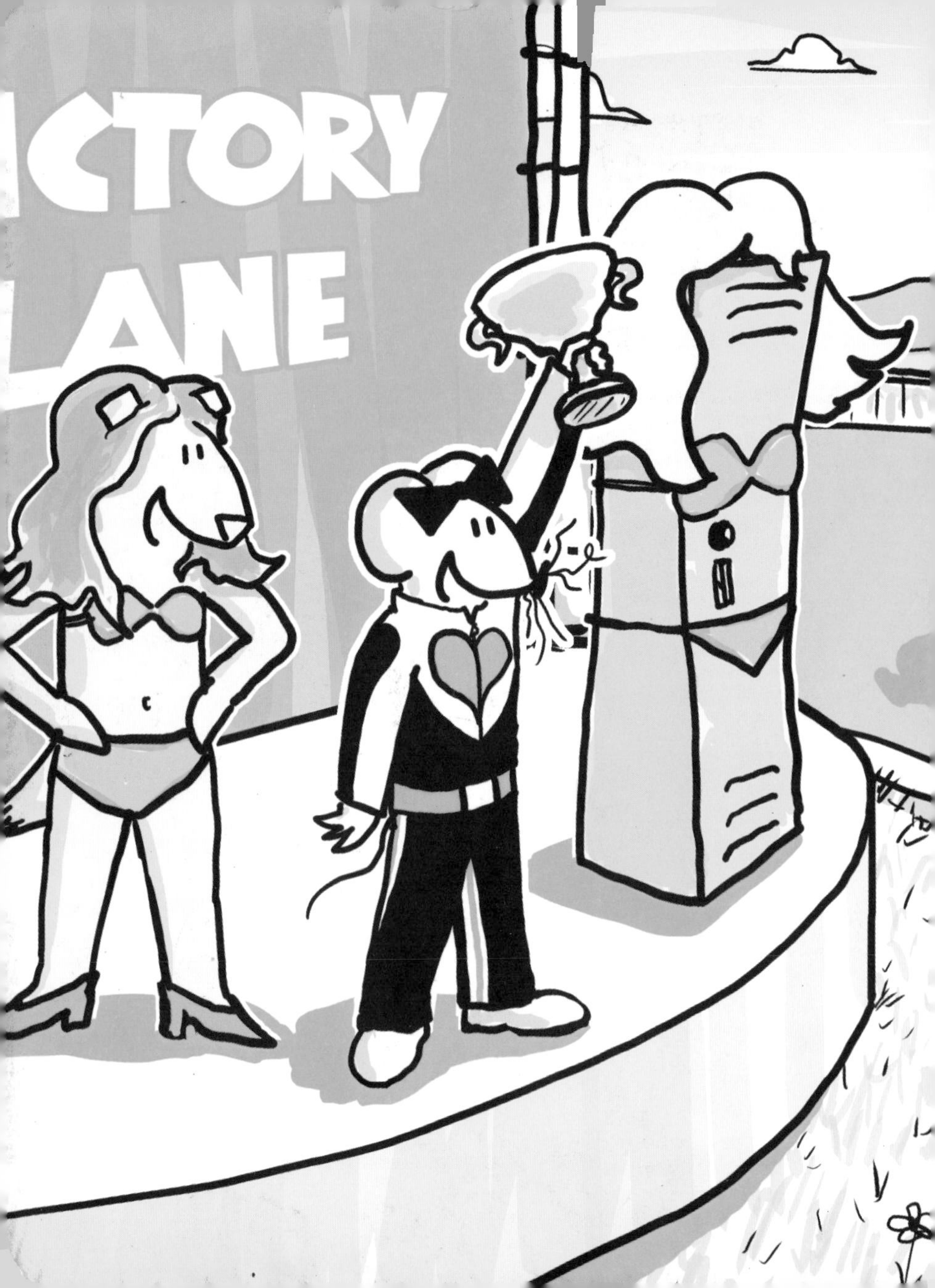
ICTORY
LANE

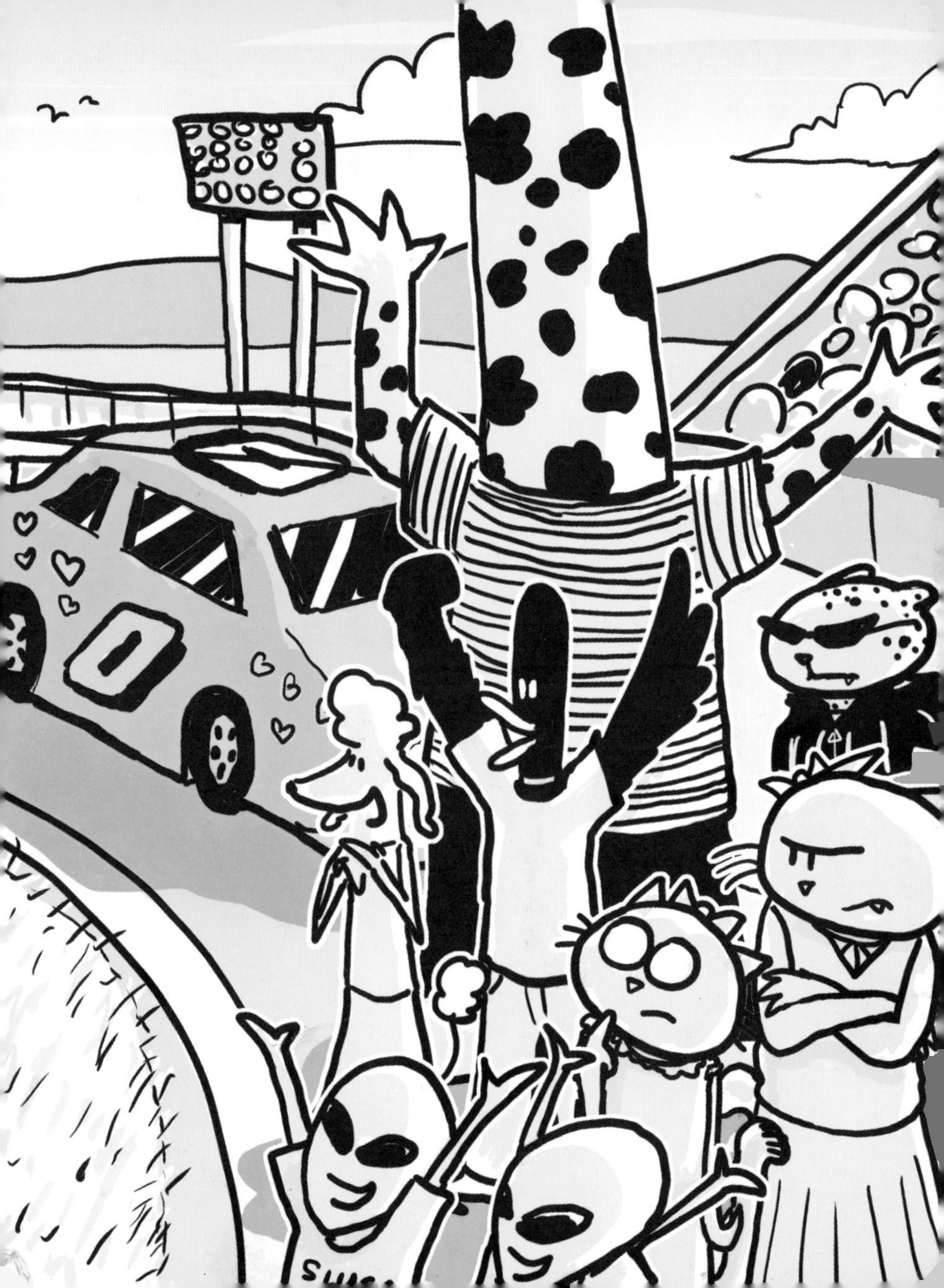
0

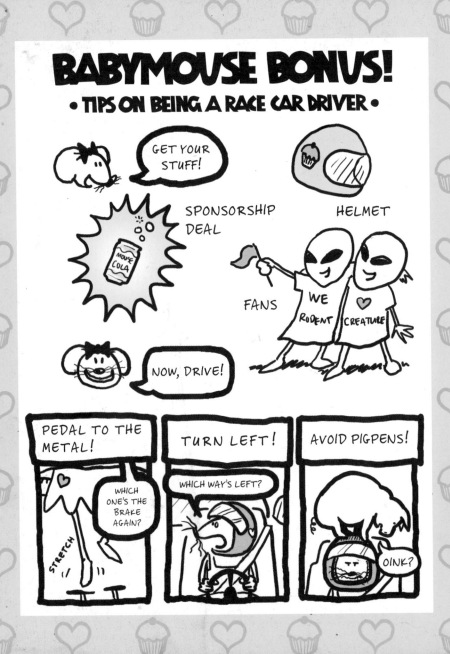